Haunts and Howls and Dragon Tales

Kat Simons

T&D PUBLISHING

Haunts and Howls and Dragon Tales

To all my favorite dragons…
Fierce and fantastic, the lot of you.

INTRODUCTION

I have been obsessed with dragons for as long as I can remember. They rank right up there with dolphins as the beastie I loved most in my youth. Dragons are what got me into reading science fiction and fantasy, first with the Dragon Riders of Pern by Anne McCafferey, and after that a Barbara Hambly novel called *Dragonsbane*. Before those books, I was all about horror and vampires. But once I started down the dragon path, I was well and truly caught.

Some of my earliest fiction, my initial attempts at short stories, were tales of dragons. One of the first story I ever submitted for publication was called *And Then a Dragon Fell on Her House*. Believe it or not, that quirky story almost got accepted at a magazine all those many years ago (we're talking more than thirty years at this stage). It was rejected in the end because the magazine already had a dragon story—at least according to the very nice rejection letter sent to this very naïve and new writer. But that near-acceptance and the encouraging words from the editor definitely encouraged my love of writing about dragons.

The giant beasties found their way into a number of my early short fiction, including some of my sillier stories. In fact, dragons appeared so often in my early writing, that I was a little surprised to discover I actually hadn't published many books with dragons in them until the last couple of years (I'm writing this in 2025). The occasional dragon made an appearance here and there. One of my earliest fantasy romance novels, *Destiny's Seduction*, published under my Isabo Kelly pseudonym, has a dragon in it.

But full books and stories with a focus on dragons were surprisingly scarce. Outside of the occasional guest appearance in other books, the only series I had with a dragon main character was my Joan of Kerry series, featuring Joan and her companion dragon, Rory.

And then I wrote *Who Steals a Dragon…*

Okay, first I wrote a story about a Komodo dragon that got stolen. But the opening line was intriguing to me because with that line, it felt like I could write all kinds of stories in all kinds of genres. So I did. A fun little book which has six different stories about six different kinds of dragons in six different genres. It was the first time in a long time I really let myself tell *dragon focused* stories. And I was hooked.

The paranormal romance story in that collection spawned an entire series of its own. The Dragon Thief series, with shapeshifting dragons. At the same time as I started writing that series, I was also mulling a theme for this year's Haunts and Howls collection. And I thought…

Dragons.

So here we are.

As a sidenote, I was really tempted to call this collection Haunts and Howls and Dragon TAILS. And probably would have except the cover had already been done with Tales. Oops.

As I was writing the stories for this collection, I thought long and hard about putting in one of my series characters from a dragon heavy series—Joan or Kerry or Myra from the Dragon Thief series. I even asked my newsletter if anyone had a preference. In the end, I decided to write mostly new things for the collection because honestly, there are just a whole lot of dragon tales to tell. And telling a lot of different stories was pretty fun.

There is one series story in here, but it's a series

that runs through the Haunts and Howls collections rather than a dragon specific series—the Destiny Cats are back!

First up in the collection, though, is a strange sort of "dragon" story. In fact, on the surface, this one might look more like a witch story—and who doesn't love a good witch story. But be assured, there's a dragon in *For Want of a Concert Ticket*. And to say anymore would spoil the fun.

The Dragon Redistribution System was one of those stories I thought would be something else when I started it. I didn't know where it was going or how it would twist in the end. It was written during a busy period of my life and I was looking for the kind of peaceful moment the main character has in the opening of this story. What happens after that momentary peace however…

The next story in the collection has a feel to it that reminds me a bit of myth. A story that's both part of this world and takes place in a world all its own. *A Dragon of Some Kind* could have gone in a certain kind direction, but as I was writing, I realized I didn't want *that* ending. Lucky for me, my creative voice agreed. The current ending was much more satisfying for me, and I hope readers will feel the same.

I've written stories about angry characters before, especially when I was experiencing a great deal of anger myself. *They Call Her Anger* is one of those (and maybe a little on the nose?). With an interesting twist. I suspect some readers will get where my anger was coming from when I put this story to the page. Some of that anger found its way into the next story as well. *Dragon Appreciation Day* introduces a narrator whose anger is colder. More contained. And has found a very specific outlet. Or has it? Do you trust her to tell you the tale?

The second to last story in the collection is one of my favorites—if an author can be said to actually *have* a favorite among their literary babies. Readers old enough to remember the *Twilight Zone* and *Strange Tales* TV series might recognize one of the inspirations for this one. I can't get more specific without ruining the story, but one very specific episode definitely played a part in the cocktail of ideas that went into creating *Imagining Things*. Another element arose from my rather complicated relationship with my own imagination. I make my living with my imagination, with my ability to create things in vivid detail and realism in my head. Putting those thoughts and fictions onto the page is the way I deal with even some of the things I'd rather not be thinking about. I wondered if that would ever come out in a story. And in this one, it did.

Finally, our newest Destiny Cats novella! Writing *Lightning Through the Cats Eyes* reminded me a little of the *Stargate* vibe. A hint of science fiction blended with something that's really mostly fantasy. When I wrote the first Destiny Cats story in the first Haunts and Howls collection (*Destiny Through the Cats Eyes* and *Haunts and Howls and Guardian Spells* respectively), I didn't realize it would become a staple of these collections. But I have really been enjoying revisiting these characters and expanding a little at a time on this world. And I have to say, I just *love* Erica. Watching her adapt to this new life, watching the way she and Galahad dance around each other… Just delicious.

Each story in here introduces a slightly different variation on the idea of dragon. Some a little more literal than others but all with a blend of the fantastic, the scary, and the mysterious. I hope readers will enjoy the journey and find stories they can really savor inside these pages.

Happy Reading!

Kat Simons
November 2025

For Want of a Concert Ticket

Chapter One

Trying to get tickets to a sold-out concert in the very swanky Vegas hotel complex should not have resulted in a magical explosion that had Mary hiding behind an overturned conference room table.

But here she was.

Hiding behind a big round conference room table, laying on its side, the cushioned chairs scattered across a—strictly in her opinion—gaudy blue and purple patterned carpet, with the remains of the conference lunch—something she'd assumed was chicken and potatoes—scattered across the floor. The chicken blended in with the white and gold lines threading through the carpet's swirling pattern which was going to be a bitch for anyone who had to clean this up later.

Though, whoever had to clean this up later was going to have bigger things to worry about than the chicken.

Like the giant swirling vortex of power circling above the speaker's podium, near the otherwise beautiful ceiling with its elaborate crown molding. The recessed lights were out, dropping the conference room into a darkness lit only by the swirling blue lights of the vortex. The disco effect made Mary's head hurt.

All she'd wanted were concert tickets. Just a couple of tickets. The Playland Hotel complex in Las Vegas was the last stop on Aaron Yin's world tour. Mary loved Aaron Yin. And since she was here anyway for the witches' conference, she'd just wanted to take this chance to see one of her favorite singers live. Really, that shouldn't have been too much to ask.

A lightning bolt zipped out of the vortex, slamming into one of the many overturned tables scattered chaotically around the large room, sending splinters of wood and charred bits of chicken flying. The stench of burnt chicken did not offset the smell of sharp ozone and the snapping electrical scent of the swirling magic.

Fortunately, most of the people who'd been in the room had fled the minute the vortex started to open. Since this wasn't the room the witches were supposed to be in, the mundane people who had been here to celebrate the exciting advancements in the insurance business were not really prepared for the vortex.

Mary half wondered what effect this experience would have on their assessment of insurance policies for big conferences going forward.

Unfortunately, there was still three insurance people trapped near the vortex. And there was the creator of the vortex still to deal with.

Mary lunged from one overturned table to another, just as power slammed into the table she'd been crouched behind. Shattered wood, porcelain, and glass sprayed everywhere. Mary hit the floor hard on her side, covering her head instinctively.

When the explosion settled, she looked up. One less conference room table. Few more cuts on her hands and arms. But so far, the little knicks and hits she'd been taking from flying debris weren't drawing much blood.

The blood was helpful, though. She was going to need it.

Another explosion, across the room from her current shelter, started a small fire in the middle of the gaudy blue carpet. The magical flames mimicked the pattern on the carpet, rising in a swirl of blue and purple with some gold and white dancing through the flames. The overhead sprinkler system didn't detect the magic fire as actual fire so didn't activate. Damn it.

Mary pulled at her own power, whispered a water spell, and flung her hand toward the flames. An aluminum bucket of water formed over the fire and dumped a steady flow of water onto it. A flow that went on much longer than the water that should have been in a bucket that size.

The magical flames sputtered and shrank. But a few sparks shot off from the main blaze and danced across a chair, catching the tan cushions on fire, too.

Mary sent another bucket of water to stop that flare up. Then had to hope the flames went out.

Because a shout from the front of the room required her full attention.

Chapter Two

The three remaining insurance people who hadn't escaped when the vortex opened were crouched behind a big, round table that was smacked up against the podium dais at the front of the long conference room. The angle of the table kept them blocked from the vortex, but it also put their backs to the stretch of wall behind the podium and gave them no clear escape route.

All the doors in the room were at one side of the long, rectangular space. And the three remaining insurance people were at the opposite side of the room.

The only saving grace in all this was that the conference room was an interior one, so at least there were no windows for curious onlookers from the surrounding hotels in the complex to get a good look at the magical disaster happening in the room.

Mary studied the vortex from around the side of her own covering table. Swirling blue light around a blackhole center from which another blast of magical power arrowed out, slamming into a defenseless chair.

She couldn't close that thing from here. She'd need to be closer.

And even if she could shut it down on her own —which was not guaranteed—she'd still have Deborah to deal with.

Bitch couldn't just let it go. Just had to prove how powerful she was. Had to start shit when all Mary had been trying to do was get concert tickets.

Deborah should never have been invited to the witches gathering in the first place. Even her snack contributions were subpar.

Mary snorted. Then ducked again when another volley of magical lightning raced over her head.

Come to a conference. We'll have some good times. Exchange a few spells.

The three insurance people screamed as one of the bolts hit a server's cart only a few feet away. The explosion sent porcelain plateware and leftover chicken slamming into the wall at one side of the room, dripping black, burnt detritus down the pale walls.

Damn it. She had to get them out of here. Without the remaining mundanes, she could take care of the vortex. And Deborah.

She scrambled around the dubious cover of overturned tables. Crouched behind an upturned chair. And used a dropped silver drinks tray to catch some of the wild magic, tossing it back toward the vortex.

The magic slid into the central whirling blackness with a noise like metal scraping across paper—a sound that gave Mary the chills.

She reached the cowering insurance people just as another volley of powerful bolts ricocheted around the conference room.

Two women and a man. The man screamed when Mary rolled to cover behind the table.

Mary rose to a crouch and raised her hands in a calming gesture. "One of the good guys," she said. "Here to get you out."

"What the hell is going on? Did you do this?" the man demanded, his gruff tone doing nothing to hide his terror.

He was middle aged, maybe in his mid-forties to early-fifties, wearing a decent suit that looked like off-the-rack but tailored to fit his lean body. His blond hair was thinning and the tanning he'd done had created creases around his blue eyes.

"What's going on is complicated and we don't

have time for explanations," Mary said, avoiding the "did you do this" question. Technically, she hadn't opened the vortex. But that was a technicality she didn't have time to explain.

One of the two women was youngish, in her twenties, and wearing a red pants suit that seemed very bold compared to most of the other, more conservative black and gray suits Mary had seen on the escaping insurance people. The young woman's black hair was cut in a little bob that showed off excellent cheekbones. And her makeup had probably been flawless but there were now streaks of black mascara tracking down her cheeks from her tears.

The other woman was older than the rest, approaching her sixties, maybe older, her white hair pulled back into what had probably once been a slick bun but was now listing to one side. She'd dropped her suit jacket somewhere and only had on a pink silk shirt and a fitted gray skirt. She'd dropped her shoes along the way as well, which, if they'd been heels, Mary thought showed good forethought. The only glass or sharp things on the carpet were from broken dinnerware and glassware, but there were no windows to shatter. And running away in heels would have been a lot harder than avoiding the areas with broken glass.

The older woman held the younger woman's

hand and absently patting it as she rolled her eyes at the man. "Don't bother about him," she said. "He's just scared—"

"I am not!" the man insisted.

The older woman ignored him. "How do we get out of here?" She looked past Mary toward the doors. "That's a long way to go."

From their position at the far end of the room, right next to the swirling vortex, the exit doors did absolutely look very far away.

Mary glanced at the vortex as another bolt of magic lightning streaked out to slam into the carpet on the opposite side of the room.

"Okay, she said, facing the three insurance people again. "I'm going to create a shield. Don't ask." She pointed a finger at the man when he opened his mouth. "No time. Once it's up, run to the doors there to the left. They'll get you back out into the main hallway. Hotel staff should be waiting for you."

Mary had had to bespell the doors so none of the staff tried to get in to help.

This wasn't something hotel security could deal with, even if they were the best in Vegas. And that would only give Mary more mundanes she'd have to rescue.

Time she didn't have if she wanted to get the vortex closed before it was too late.

As if in answer to her worry, a noise boomed out from inside the vortex. A noise like a growl and a screech had had a baby. A noise that wasn't anything humans in this realm heard.

The sound made the hairs on Mary's arm rise.

Shit shit shit.

The draken was coming.

Chapter Three

Mary scrambled to form the shield spell, a combination of words and applied magic that would keep the three insurance people safe from random shots of magic as they made their escape. Shield spells were fast spells, but took a lot of magic. And she was going to need at least some of that magic sooner than it would take for her to rebuild it without outside help.

She glanced to the left, at the swirling black hole of bluish magic. To the darkness at its center. Her gut tightened and her whole body trembled.

The draken was coming. If it got out into this realm from the void, it would destroy not just this conference room or the hotel beyond, it would wreak havoc on the entire hotel complex. Might even destroy all of Vegas before the witches gathered here could contain it.

Hell, even with the conference attendees, there might not be enough witches to send the draken back.

Damn it, Deborah. Just had to win. Couldn't just sit the fuck down.

Mary finished the shield spell, throwing it up in a line that ran the length of the conference room. It wove around fallen tables and chairs, grounding into the carpeted floor so no rogue magic could slip beneath it. She had it raised to the ceiling too, but there were spaces in the elaborate crown molding that might let magic slip past, so she had to get the innocent bystanders out.

"Now," she shouted. "Run. Straight to the door. Do not stop. Do not look back. Go."

The older woman didn't even hesitate. She grabbed the younger woman's arm, hauled her to her feet and ran for the door. Fast enough Mary had a feeling the older woman was a runner in the real world. The younger woman, who'd never even spoken, stumbled along behind her. To be fair, the young woman managed to run in her gorgeous spiked heels a lot better than Mary would have.

The man was last to leave. He looked at the vortex, looked at Mary. "I should…stay and help." He swallowed hard.

"No," Mary assured, settling a hand on his arm. "This isn't a fight you understand. It's okay to leave it to an expert." Not that she was an expert in void magic, but she knew more than the insurance man. "It's okay. I've got this."

He nodded, hesitated a moment more.

The draken's screeching growl erupted from the depths of the void darkness.

The man jumped, and finally took off toward the doors, ducking as he ran, covering his head with his hands as if he expected something deadly to rain out of the ceiling.

Not a bad instinct given what was just the other side of that vortex.

Once the three insurance people dove through the doors at the far side of the conference room, Mary quickly reformed a locking spell, sealing everyone out.

And hopefully, sealing the draken inside the conference room if it escaped the void.

Mary finally turned back to the vortex.

The slipstream of blue light swirling around the central blackness might have been pretty if it hadn't opened onto a realm so deadly it could swallow her world whole.

The vortex didn't look to be growing, which was a blessing, but that wouldn't stop the draken from escaping. A pinhole opening into the void was enough for a draken to snake into this world.

Which was why no witch in her right mind opened a vortex into the void. Especially as just a fucking distraction.

Mary looked at the various nicks and cuts on her bare arms and hands. The smaller bleeds had already stopped and were clotting, but there were a couple of larger gashes. Blood leaked out of those. Not much, but enough she could dampen her fingers in the thick redness.

When she felt like there was enough on all of her fingertips, she faced the vortex and raised her hands, chanting the spell she *thought* would close the swirling portal. She wrote the runes of the spell on the air, the magic filtering through her own blood to create visible symbols in golden light.

For a tension-filled moment, the vortex remained exactly as it was, neither shrinking nor growing. Swirling. Another bolt of power shooting from the central void.

The draken's screech, nearer now.

Then… Almost imperceptible at first. There! There. Shrinking. The swirling blue light, an accretion disk around the void center, slowly pulling inward, slowly winding down.

Three rapid shots of power burst from the shrinking center, burning holes into the blue and purple carpet and the surrounding air. The stench of melted polyester and burnt ozone filled the conference room. The heat from the shot made Mary sweat.

A fire erupted to her right, the blue flames dancing in her peripheral vision. Couldn't stop to put those out yet. Damn it.

The vortex swirled smaller.

Another blast of power shot from the very center of the void, barreling right for Mary. She couldn't move, couldn't duck away or she risked breaking the spell that was closing the vortex.

She winced, prepared to take the hit, hoped it wasn't one of the magical bolts that would burn…

Chapter Four

A round silver disk, a server's drinks tray, rose in front of Mary, catching the magical void bolt inches before it hit her.

She blinked as the shot ricocheted to the left, smashing a toppled chair into splinters.

Ouch.

She winced again. Then faced her rescuer.

The older woman who'd supposedly just escaped with the other two insurance people.

"I'll ask how you got back in here in a few minutes," Mary said, facing the shrinking vortex again. "Thanks for your help."

"Welcome. You need more blood."

The woman was right. The golden runes in front of the vortex had faded, glowing less brightly now.

The blood on Mary's fingertips had nearly melted away, all of it gone into the spell.

But the vortex wasn't closed yet.

And it had stopped shrinking as the runes faded.

Damn it. She hunted the various nicks and cuts on her arms, but her infernal ability to heal well from small injuries foiled her hopes. Most of her cuts were scabbed over now. Only dried blood on her skin, which wasn't helpful.

She needed fresh blood on her fingertips.

"Don't suppose you have a knife to hand?" she asked even as she hunted the floor for fallen cutlery. She didn't think the bland chicken that had been served for lunch had needed sharp knives but maybe it had since the chicken looked more like rubber than food.

"Here," the woman said, tapping something against Mary's arm.

Mary glanced down to see a silver athame with a beautifully bejeweled hilt and a thick, short blade. A very sharp blade.

"I'd give you some of my blood, but you've already started the spell," the woman said.

There was a part of Mary processing this, recognizing that this woman whom she'd assumed was a mundane insurance person was actually a practicing witch, even though she hadn't apparently been here for the witches conference—Mary didn't recognize her anyway—but she was too worried about the vortex to think about these facts too closely.

If they survived this, she did have questions.

"What's your name?" she asked as she took the athame.

"Norma," the woman said.

"Thanks, Norma. I'm Mary."

Mary slid the sharpened blade across her inner left forearm, sucking in a breath at the sting. Blood welled in the cut. She quickly handed the short dagger back to the woman and dipped her fingertips into the blood, rubbing them together, rubbing more blood into her fingertips on her left hand.

Then she raised her hands and reformed the fading runes, infusing them with power.

The spike in the spell restarted the vortex's shrinking. It whirled faster, closing down on itself.

Beyond the vortex, another screech from the draken. A sound that Mary felt in her bones.

"Did the ground just shake?" Norma asked.

"'Fraid so." Mary grunted. She pushed more power through her fingers, into the runes, into the spell.

The vortex shrank. Shrank.

Something slid past the opening, on the other side of the vortex, a dark, glittering expanse of spiked scales.

Mary swallowed hard.

"Gotta get that closed," Norma said, her voice breathy and hollow.

"Yup. Working on it."

She flowed more power into the spell. Panic had her heartbeat hammering. Sweat dripped down her back. She tightened her hold on the spell, sent more magic through her blood covered fingertips.

The runes flashed bright gold.

The vortex shrank.

Another slide of those glittering sharp scales across the open blackness of the void.

A screech that shook the entire room.

Mary grunted and threw more magic into her spell. This time, however, something pushed back.

Something...*resisted.*

CHAPTER FIVE

Mary slid backward, her knees rubbing through her dress slacks against the rough carpet. Horror filled her. No. No no no no! She couldn't let the draken get through. If it entered this realm, it would destroy everything.

Norma leaned up behind her, keeping Mary upright and in place. Another shove from inside the void, an invisible hand pressed against Mary's face. Thanks to the extra support from Norma, she didn't slide backward again. But the push hurt.

Created the kind of pressure that could crush bones.

"Not good," she muttered. The stench of burnt ozone nearly choked her now.

"I've got you," Norma said. "I've got the fires behind us out. You focus on that vortex."

Mary hadn't even realized the fires behind her had been that bad. She only noticed the smoke circling around the air in front of her after Norma mentioned it.

She redoubled her efforts, pouring all the magic she had to hand through the blood on her fingertips, called on the blood in her veins to aid her, dragged in what magic she could from the environment around her.

Chanting the spell again, adding the power of her voice to it, she sank everything she had into the closing the vortex.

Another invisible force slammed against her. The slide of black, glittering scales across the void made her tremble. A smell of burnt electricity, bitter minerals, and something fishy oozed from the void.

The scales shifted, slithered…

And a huge red eye came into view.

The red glowed, with lines of black light streaking through the color, and a long narrow pupil. The eye flickered, like a blink. A growl joined that eye flicker.

A scream clawed at Mary's throat. She channeled it into the spell, pushing everything she had left.

The vortex swirled tighter, closing until there

was only a small circle of space left, no larger than the drinks trays. Even the blue light around the vortex tightened, forming a bright blue line swirling too fast for her eyes to track.

The draken's eye bulged through the hole, pushing against the barrier. The pressure built inside Mary until she felt like her bones really were being crushed. A scream finally escaped as she threw all her remaining strength into the spell.

Watched the vortex resist the pressure from both directions.

And then, with the most sickeningly gross popping sound Mary had ever heard…

The vortex snapped shut.

CHAPTER SIX

The ear-piercing sound of the draken's denial echoed in the conference room for seconds after the vortex closed.

For a long moment, Mary knelt, panting, staring at the spot where the vortex had been. She trembled, blinking back spots as the rush of adrenaline and blood magic left her about to collapse. Her ears felt stuffed with cotton and the pressure in her head made her feel like she'd surfaced from scuba diving too fast. That was going to bring on one hell of a headache later.

When she got the trembling under control enough she felt like she could maneuver her own limbs without help, she scooted around to face Norma.

The older woman's bun had completely

collapsed at this point, her white hair tumbling down too her shoulders in waves, little fly-away hairs spiking around her face. Her brown eyes were wide as she stared at the spot where the vortex had been, and the hand she still had gripping Mary's arm shook.

"Well, that was…" Mary started.

"Terrifying," Norma finished.

"Absolutely terrifying."

Norma blinked a few times and looked at Mary. "Thank you for closing that. I couldn't. Tried, but I didn't have the power."

"Kind of raises some questions there," Mary said. "You *are* here for the insurance conference, right?"

Norma nodded. "That's my day job. Witching is the other significant part of my life. But when the witches conference and the business conference overlapped, I had to make a choice. My boss was going to be here, and I didn't want her to see me at a different conference and start asking questions. She's…not the type to believe in the supernatural."

"She might have changed her mind after this." Mary gestured vaguely at the now destroyed conference room. "Deborah has a lot to answer for," she muttered.

"Deborah? Isn't she that witch that always

brings really bad snacks to any meeting she attends?"

"That's the one!" And now Mary wondered why she'd never met Norma before if they were both aware of Deborah's horrible snacks. Probably just missed each other over the years. Mary supposed she couldn't know *every* witch that existed.

"What's Deborah have to do with this?" Norma asked.

They both scanned the conference room. Burnt chicken and potatoes slid down the cream walls and dripped off the ceiling's beautiful crown molding. The blue purple carpet was melted and charred. Every table and chair upturned or obliterated. The stench of ozone and burnt plastic almost overpowering the fried electrical, bitter mineral, fishy stench of the draken.

"I'm glad my company doesn't do the insurance for this place," Norma murmured.

"I just wanted concert tickets," Mary said with a sigh.

"What concert?"

"Aaron Yin."

"How did that lead to this?"

"The concert is sold out, but there was another witch who had a ticket she wasn't going to use. Deborah and I both wanted it. I offered more money. The witch was going to give me the ticket. And

Deborah opened the vortex in a mundane human's conference room to distract me so she could go snatch the ticket instead."

"That's…" Norma shook her head. "That's twisted."

"Diabolical," Mary agreed.

"Deborah is going to need a good talking to," Norma said. "And someone needs to strip her of her powers for a month for this kind of chaos."

"I'll talk to the conference organizers. At the very least, they can ban her from future gatherings." Mary let out a sigh. "At least the draken didn't get out and no one was hurt. Shame about all the witnesses, though."

"There's a hotel full of witches," Norma said. "We should be able to come up with some excuse and bespell our way out of this."

"I'm thinking a gas explosion might do it."

"Or a short in the electrical system. Put on a pretty good light display."

"That is an excellent excuse," Mary said, giving Norma an admiring smile.

"Not my first rodeo," she said with a grin. She climbed up to her still bare feet and put out a hand to help Mary stand. The process was a little wobbly because Mary had the energy reserves of an exhausted toddler at that moment. But she managed to stay on her feet.

"And speaking of," Norma said, "I made a trade with a colleague, gave them a pair of tickets I had to the rodeo this weekend in exchange for their concert tickets."

Mary's eyes widened, even though she tried to keep her excitement in check. "Concert?"

"I love Aaron Yin. Last chance to see him before the end of his tour." Norma smiled. "Got an extra ticket. Want to join me?"

Mary squealed and gave Norma a hug, glad all her various cuts had clotted and scabbed over already so she didn't get blood and Norma's pretty pink blouse. Quick healing and concert tickets for the win!

This was not the path she would have chosen to get concert tickets. But she'd take 'em. And her new friend.

As they headed out, she glanced at the spot where the vortex had been. She finally understood that whole "What happens in Vegas, stays in Vegas" thing.

Because this really needed to stay in Vegas.

The Dragon Redistribution System

Chapter One

On the other side of the valley there's a hill, and behind that hill there's a cave, and inside that cave there's a dragon. The dragon isn't a real dragon. Or, well, if it is, it's a dead dragon. The dragon is a collection of stone that *look* like a dragon. The rocks are shaped and curved on the floor of the cave to look like the body, neck, and head of a dragon that is roughly the length of a semitruck and about as thick.

There are legends about the rocks that look like a dragon. Stories told by kids all over the area. When I was growing up, the kids at school used to talk about how the dragon was cursed and turned into stone by a witch. Kids from another school claimed the dragon had fallen asleep for so long it had petrified and would wake up again one day. And at my husband's school, he said the kids believed the dragon had just grown old and died and that's what happened to dead dragons.

One thing everyone agreed on, though, was that the dragon was dead—and of course all the kids agreed that the dragon *had* been real at one stage—and that whatever treasure the dragon had hoarded had been stolen a long time ago. But! But there was still, supposedly, some of it still hidden under the dragon. And if you could move that stone dragon out of the way, there'd be treasure there.

Not that any of the kids tried. It would literally take breaking apart a semitruck's worth of solid gray continental rock. And outside of no one really wanting to destroy the dragon, I'd always heard whispers that to break the stone would wake the dragon again. A dragon loose on the mountains in modern times seemed like a bad idea. Even to silly teenagers.

So when I found myself in this cave in my forties, the last thing I expected to see was the dragon damaged.

At first, I didn't even notice. I'd been hiking through the woods, alone because work was stressful and I needed some time away from… Well, everything. Technology, husband, neighbors, news… Life. Things were fine, really. Nothing horrible. No deaths in the family. My husband and I weren't fighting. Only minor financial stress. His mother was getting sicker. That was going to be an issue soon. Work was horrible, but it was that time of year. Tax time and I was an accountant so…

The spring had started to bring warmer weather a little early, and I was desperate for some nature and some quiet. So I drove across the valley to the hill with the dragon's cave and went for a gentle hike through the pines. It was really rejuvenating. Really helped get me out of my own head.

So I wasn't really thinking when the clouds moved overhead and the little patters of rain started to hit the rich dirt and pine needles. The smell of all that rain and pine and dirt was soothing and refreshing, but I hadn't brought a change of clothes with me so I didn't want to get soaked. It was still chilly enough just the thought of getting that wet was miserable. Since the dragon's cave was close, I'd jogged to it and taken refuge just before the downpour.

For a long while, I stood at the mouth of the cave, watching the rain sheet down, watching it blur the trees and turn the landscape into a dripping watercolor painting of greens and browns. Almost a meditation watching that transformation, listening to the rain pound the dirt and trees, the quiet behind me in the cave, breathing in the clean water and damp earth. The cave had a faintly musty smell. The cool, coldness of stone that's been undisturbed for a long time. I wondered if kids still came out here to visit the dragon. We had when I was younger, but that was a different time. We didn't have a lot of fun devices and gaming consols and tablets and tiny computers in our hands to distract us.

After a while of quietly watching the rain, I turned to inspect the cave. I hadn't been up here myself in probably twenty-five years, so there was that moment of nostalgia mixing with the current reality. The memories from my teenage years superimposed over the current view.

Not much had changed. It was a relatively empty cave. There wasn't much here that *could* change. Tall enough I'd have had to climb the dragon rocks to reach the ceiling and still stand on my toes to do it. Deep enough that the very back of the cave was pitch black, and would have been even if the day hadn't gotten darker with the sudden storm. When I'd been here as a teenager, I remembered going to the very back of the cave with flashlights to see the dragon's "tail." There was one, too. A very long slender bit of rock that sort of curled on itself and looked like an actual dragon tail.

We'd brought the flashlights and gone exploring thinking we might find some hidden treasure, which, of course, wasn't there. But we'd had fun climbing over the rocks and looking for hidden doors or secret crevices. The rear of the cave was smooth and empty, though. Not even any piles of rocky debris to hide things under. Nothing but a bare stone floor and a curved smooth wall all the way up to the ceiling.

There weren't even any stalactites in here, which probably should have been surprising because there was a lot of moisture in these mountains. The cave was open enough for the cold winds to scour everything flat apparently. Except, of course, for the dragon.

This visit, I had a phone flashlight, which frankly wasn't as strong as my dad's old steal tube of a light, but it fought back the gloom. I studied the dragon's head and neck, still curved with the big wedge-shaped rock that was the head, its "nose" pointed toward the front of the cave and the neck rock arched around. The body was a thicker, tall rock with some smaller cuts and boulders beside it that passed for legs and, if you looked right, wings pressed against the body.

I'd had an easier time seeing the "wings" when I was a kid. Now, looking at the giant boulder, I had to move the flashlight around a lot and look at the rock from the corner of my eye before I could spot the cuts and lines of silvery minerals that gave the appearance of wings.

The wind shifted directions. When I glanced back, the rain was slashing into the front of the cave now, soaking the spot I'd previously been standing and bringing in damp coldness that I wasn't dressed for. I shivered and moved deeper into the cave, using my phone's flashlight to guide me. It looked like I'd be there for a while, so I decided to see if anything at the rear of the cave had changed.

The back was just as smoothing and featureless as I remembered. Or at least mostly. There did seem to be a pile of pine needles and grass and rocks that had blown up against the rear wall and not blown back out of the cave yet. The swirling air had bundled all the debris into a pile not far from the dragon's tail.

Just like I had when I was a kid, I ran my hand along the back wall, looking for secret passages, and hidden nooks. I didn't believe I'd find anything —if generations of kids hadn't found anything yet, there was nothing here to find. My exploration brought me closer to the dragon's tail and the pile of debris just as a huge gust of wind arrowed into the cave, howling around me like a banshee. I ducked behind the rocky tail to avoid the swirling chaos as it kicked up the pile of dead leaves and twigs and brought in more pine needles and grass. The wind tugged at my hair, pulling it loose from the ponytail, and nearly made off with my baseball cap.

When everything settled again, I glanced around the tail. More debris had piled up in the same spot, though the pile was a little higher now. I leaned against the curved rock, straightening my ponytail and hat, and that's when I spotted the broken rocks.

On the side of the dragon closest to the cave walls, where the body rock got so close to the wall no one really went there, the space too narrow to pass between rock and wall, there was a pile of stones forming a small pyramid, and a hole in the side of the body rock. A rounded chuck taken out, like someone had come in with a rock drill and carved a half circle into the side of the dragon. The hole was rough, but shaped so spherically it couldn't have been just natural erosion or rocks just breaking off.

I tried to remember back twenty-five years to what that side of the dragon had looked like before. Had there been a section of the boulder that protruded and could have been easily knocked off? No, we definitely would have tried that as kids, thinking there might be hidden treasure. I couldn't remember any obvious flaws on that side of the rock that might have resulted in the damage happening naturally. It must have been done on purpose.

But who the hell would carve a half-sphere into the side of the dragon rocks?

When I got close enough to really see the cut, focusing my flashlight on it, the mystery deepened. I'd expected to see obvious chisel marks, straight lines to show where someone had applied a power chisel, or holes where a drill had broken the hard gray stone. But the interior didn't show anything obvious. It did glitter with the same silvery mineral that made the "wings" on the side of the dragon. I wasn't sure what the mineral was. A more geology knowledgeable friend of mine from college might have known. It did remind me of the interior of a geode, but all silver. No gold or purples or any other cool colors. The light from my flashlight caught the cuts and crystals, flashing and sparkling.

The pile of stones under the cut were a mix of the outer part of the rock and the interior geode like silver crystal-mineral stuff. Squatting down, I moved the top few stones on the pile. If I were still a teenager, I might imagine the pile looked like it had spilled out of the hole to form this pyramid. Or the pyramid had been stacked on purpose by whoever created the hole to make it look that way.

Was that it? Had somebody been trying to… create a bit of art here or something? It was possible. People used natural features to make art sometimes, didn't they?

But if that had been the case, they'd left it here to be discovered and not told anyone about it because this would definitely be something the local papers and news stations would have mentioned if it had been a purposeful installation. And it really didn't look like much, to be honest. Just a half-sphere hole and a pile of stones.

So maybe someone had gotten the clever idea to finally cut into the rock looking for treasure? Or were just curious to see what the interior of the "dragon" looked like? No way to know really. But it was odd.

I stood again and ran my fingers over the interior of the hole in the dragon's side. The rocks were rough and bumpy. But surprisingly a little sticky too. When I pulled my fingers back, there was a smear of black on them, like ink. I had no idea what that might be. The gray and silver interior didn't look to have anything on it that would rub away black.

A quick sniff hit me in the face with a tar and rotten eggs scent. I'd never come across anything that was quite that combination before. And it wasn't pleasant. Maybe it was tar from whatever machine had been used to make the hole. Whatever it was, I didn't want to wipe it off on my jeans and spend the rest of the day walking around with that smell on me, so I wiped my fingers across the cave wall, hoping to get most of the black stuff off. Then I used one of the half-full water bottles in my backpack to rinse the rest of the gunk off. It mostly came away, but I could still smell it if I brought my hands close to my face.

That was going to take soap and water to really get the smell off. I considered holding my hand out to the rain still pouring down in front of the cave mouth, but it was coming down so hard it almost looked like I was standing at the back of a waterfall. If I got too close, I'd probably end up soaked, which would defeat the purpose of coming into the cave to begin with.

I had checked the weather report before coming up here today. And there'd been nothing about a strong storm like this blowing through. But sometimes the weather in the mountains, especially in the spring, could be unpredictable, so I knew I just had to wait it out.

The thicker the rain got, though, the darker the cave felt. And the wind that kept gusting in with noisy howls and echoes was cold. My flannel overshirt, which I'd wrapped around my waist during the hike, wasn't really up to the chill in the air like a jacket would have been. Reminder to self to include a raincoat even on sunny hiking days.

I buttoned the flannel closed and went hunting for a spot in the cave that gave some protection from the wind. The area inside the rocky curve of the dragon's tail kept most of the chill and swirling gusts away, so I sat down, set my backpack aside, leaned back against the rock, and prepared to wait out the storm.

Chapter Two

I must have dozed off to the whistle of wind and rain because I blinked my eyes open suddenly when I heard a scraping sound. Considering I was sitting on a cold stone floor with my back to more cold stone, I was surprised to realize I wasn't chilled. In fact, I was quite comfortably warm. It took a few minutes of blinking awake to realize the stone at my back wasn't actually cold. It was warm. Soothing. Like sitting next to a fire. Which was weird.

The scraping sound again.

Sitting up straight I looked around. Probably an animal that had come in to get out of the rain, too, but if it was something big like a bear or mountain lion, I was going to be in trouble. I moved slowly, almost holding my breath, as I stood and looked over the top of the curved rock. My eyes had adjusted to the dark and I was looking from my dark spot out toward the muted gray light coming in through the cave mouth, so I had a good view of the central part of the cave.

But there was nothing there.

Nothing as big as a bear or cougar, thank goodness, but also nothing small like a raccoon or squirrel or even a bird. Just the open cavern floor around the rocks of the dragon's body. The plant debris that had blown up against the back wall wasn't swirling around—the wind had stopped blowing directly into the cave while I'd snoozed—so that wasn't the source of the scraping noise.

Weird.

I leaned against the rocky tail and hunted the darker portions of the cavern, looking for something moving near where the wall met the floor maybe, and then up thinking maybe it might be a bat or a bird up high. But the noise had been coming from closer to ground level. I hadn't heard it above my head.

Thankfully because the thought freaked me out a little. I wasn't afraid of bats. I liked them. They ate bugs and were very cute. But I would have been bothered by one flying over my head when I wasn't prepared for or aware of them. And since I couldn't be sure if a bat bit me while I was snoozing, I'd have to go get rabies shots. Which would suck.

Fortunately, nothing overhead, though. But without the flashlight to see into the dark edges of the cave, I couldn't see anything that might be responsible for the noise. Nothing moved as I watched.

I was a little afraid to turn on the flashlight and startle some animal that might be dangerous. And the thought of something slithering suddenly or jumping at me because I startled it was not comforting.

I watched quietly for a long time, straining to hear the sounds of scraping I'd heard before, trying to get a better idea of the direction. The rain sounded less severe outside now. But still coming down steadily. The rocks under my hands were surprisingly warm, but that was probably because the winds weren't icing the inside of the cave anymore, and I'd been leaning on the stone long enough for my body heat to warm it up a little.

When nothing moved and I didn't hear any more scraping, I relaxed. Probably just some of the grass and sticks moving. Even if I hadn't seen anything. It was dark back here. My eyesight was adjusted to the dimness but still just ordinary human eyesight.

Turning around, I thought I'd slide down the tail to the ground again and maybe snooze some more.

There was still too much rain to leave so might as well go back to being somewhat comfortable. But as I started to ease down to the floor, a flash of brightness like light in front of me had me stilling. My brain took several beats to catch up, but once it did, I stopped breathing. Not light. Eyes. Two large eyes, winking at me in the dimness, bright enough to glow. Purple and red eyes. With a cat-slit pupil.

I sucked in a gasp of air when I realized I was going to pass out from not breathing, but I couldn't move otherwise. Slowly, slowly, my attention expanded to take in the animal surrounding those strange eyes.

Gray and green. Scales. The length of my forearm. Four legs with little padded toes that clung to the side of the cave wall. That's where the creature was, clinging to the side of the cave wall. Staring right at me with its weird purple and red eyes. The gray and green scales actually blended in with the rocks, so it took a minute for me to see the long tail stretching away from the already long body. A tail tipped with tiny, needle thin spikes that looked like they'd hurt if I got anywhere near them.

The tail was angled upward, but also plastered to the wall. It looked like the…what was it? A lizard? An iguana? Had been crawling down the wall from the roof to position itself at my head level to look at me. It flickered out a long, forked tongue, furthering my assumption that it was a giant lizard of some kind. And it let out a quiet hiss of sound like a pipe slowly releasing steam. A steady stream of sound interrupted only briefly when it flickered its tongue to taste the air.

There were also thicker spines along its back which were laid flat but looked like they could rise into a row of protective and dangerous spears if necessary. More needle thin spikes with a thin greenish membrane surrounded the lizard's head, also laid flat but with the look of something that could puff up like a mane.

Its wedge-shaped nose was long, raised nostrils that reminded her of a crocodile, and some eye teeth sticking out from the closed mouth like little white grains of rice stuck to his scaled lips.

The impression of lizard was so strong that it took me a while before I realized that the shape of the creature's head was the same as the rock dragon's. And that there were translucent, delicate looking wings flattened to the creature's sides. Hard to say if it was two or four wings because of the way they were folded tight to the body. But definitely wings. Definitely not like any lizard I'd encountered before.

It hissed again and moved an inch down the wall.

I startled, gasping as I pressed against the rocky tail at my back. The rock was even warmer than it had been a moment before. Not quite hot, but getting there. The part of my brain not busying trying not to get bit by a lizard I couldn't identify worried about that heat. But I was too focus on trying not to get bitten or spit at by the lizard to think about it too closely. Visions of dinosaur movies and poisoned spit ran through my head. It didn't look big enough to eat me as it was, but if it paralyzed me, I was toast.

It opened its mouth, revealing a row of very sharp teeth, took several deep breaths. Terrified, I crawled over the dragon's tail to get some cover. Scrambling like my life depended on it. I got to the top of the tail just as the lizard released what it had taken that breath to release. I dropped down behind the tail, covering my head as a burst of fire shot across the rocks where I'd just been.

The lizard had breathed fire. I was not aware of any lizard in the history of lizards that could breathe fire. Only mythical things breathed fire. Mythical things like…

Dragons.

I heard some scrambling and looked up in time to see the lizard above me again, standing on the dragon tail now. I had to be imagining things. It was big but not dragon big. It had sharp teeth, but it also looked like a strange lizard. Yes, it's head was shaped like the rock dragon, but…

I had to be imagining things.

The lizard opened its mouth again and I knew I was about to be cooked. "Wait!" I held up a hand. "I'm not food!"

The lizard snapped its mouth shut. Which surprised me as much as its presences surprised me. Then it tilted its head and made this sort of cooing noise. A chirping sort of purr. Which was a strange combination of sounds, but it didn't sound threatening. It sounded curious.

Some of those dinosaurs in that movie had sounded curious too. Right before they at that guy. So I wasn't taking the cooing for granted. I eased up to my feet, hands in front of me. The little lizard tilted its head again and its tongue flickered out, tasting the air. Then it made a noise that was a sort of hissed surprise and it leapt so suddenly, I didn't even have time to gasp.

The weight of it hitting me in the chest sent us both backward. I hit the ground hard, somehow managed to keep from bashing my head by sheer will, but my back wasn't going to be the same after that. The lizard stood on my chest, that fire-breathing, teeth-filled mouth only an inch away from my face. Maybe I should have gone ahead and let my head slam into the stone floor. Then I'd be unconscious when this thing started cooking and eating me.

Somewhat to my surprise, I'd raised my hands and held the lizard as we fell, sort of protectively, my hands around its long body. The spines remained flat so I hadn't poked myself on one, thankfully. Its scales were smooth and slick and also warmer than I'd expected. Soft and subtle, not slimy like I'd assumed reptiles felt.

Now that we were face to face, and I had my hands wrapped around its body, though, I was afraid to let go. Afraid it would lunge and eat my face. I had no idea if I was even strong enough to hold the lizard back if it lunged. But it was a bit like that old story of grabbing hold of a tiger's tail. Letting go was when it ate you.

Translucent lenses flickered over the lizard's red and purple eyes, and the slit of its pupil widened. It made the cooing-purr-chirp noise again. Tasted the air with its tongue. Tilted its head one direction, then the next, inspecting me.

As calmly and quietly as my racing pulse allowed, I said, "There there. It's okay. We're not going to hurt each other, right? I'm sorry if I wasn't supposed to be in your cave. Just trying to get out of the rain."

The lizard, to my surprise, glanced at the cave mouth, at the rain still falling thick enough to blur the forest beyond. It made another little chittering noise. Then it wiggled in my hands. I tightened my grip instinctively, worried that letting it go would be very bad for my survival, but instead of trying to pull away, the lizard sort of curled around itself and settled on my stomach and chest like an overgrown cat. It watched the rain, its tongue occasionally flickering out, seemingly without a care in the world.

Uh. What was happening?

A gentle rumbling from somewhere in the center of the curled up lizard vibrated through my stomach and was surprisingly soothing.

I glanced past it at the gray shape of the rock dragon. Then back at the lizard curled on my stomach. This was very weird.

Afraid to move but knowing I could just lay there forever, I eased one hand away, slowly so I didn't startle the lizard. It glanced at me, the translucent lenses over its eyes flickering again. The movement simulated a blink, but a blink that didn't hide its eyes.

When it didn't move or attack, I eased away my other hand and held them out to the lizard in a show of weaponless I-come-in-peace that I hoped a lizard would understand.

Apparently, it did because it remained curled up on my stomach. It did taste the air again, its forked tongue flicking to the hand that I'd gotten that black stuff on. It gave another cooing sound and actually tucked its head under that hand, almost like…like a cat looking for a head scratch.

I gave it a little experimental scratch and head rub and it leaned hard into the gesture. More of the cooing-purr-chirp sound. Well. That was kind of sweet. I lay there for a long moment, scratching the lizard's head, listening to it purr, knowing it wasn't just a lizard.

Regular lizards didn't breathe fire.

I glanced over it at the dragon rocks again. Part of me expected the rocks to move, the dragon to lift its head… Something. But the rocks remained as they had always been, save for they were now radiating a low level of heat, and there'd been a cut on the other side of the rocks.

I glanced at the baby sitting on my stomach. Yeah. It was a baby. Don't ask how I knew for sure, but the signs were there. Some deep instinct said, Baby.

And not a lizard baby. This was a baby of a different sort.

The cave remained quiet as I considered this reality, considered that maybe I had hit my head and was currently unconscious. Or maybe this was my imagination and what was lying on my stomach with its wings pressed against its back and its little fire-breathing mouth tucked back as it shoved its head deeper into my hand for more scritches was *just* a lizard. A lizard that happened to breathe fire. And have wings. And look remarkably like a smaller version of the giant rocks that everyone had always said looked like a dragon.

Since it was just the two of us, I went ahead and asked, "Are you a dragon, little guy?"

The cooing noise got stronger. Another tasting of the air with its tongue. It licked the hand that had had the black stuff on it, a move that startled me. Its tongue was warm and wet and the brush of it tickled. Stronger cooing-purr.

"That stuff… Was it some kind of blood or more like amniotic fluid?"

More cooing. Which didn't answer my question.

"Is it just you? Or will there be…" I swallowed hard. The world was not ready for this. "Will there be siblings?"

Another tongue flicker and a sound that was more forlorn sounding, though I'm not sure why I thought that.

"Just you, then? Okay." I glanced at the rocks. "And…you can take care of yourself, I assume? Get food, live and grow and protect yourself without parental help?"

Since the parental unit was rock, or at least, that's what my instincts were telling me, I had to assume this worked similar to, like, baby turtles or something. The egg hatches and the offspring go about their business, no need for a parent to do anything for them. Though, the "lizard" sitting on my stomach seemed a lot less vulnerable and likely to get randomly eaten by a seagull than baby turtles rushing to the waves.

Quietly, we both watched the rain, the baby hiss-purring while I scratched around its head and neck —carefully around the spines. The cave stayed warm and comfortable. No more sharp, cold breezes howling through. The rain had filled the cave with a damp earth scent, and it took a while before I realized the baby had a scent I hadn't noticed before. Quite subtle, really, and I wouldn't have noticed it over the smells of the cave and rain and pines.

But in the quiet, with it so close, its breath puffing out of its raised nostrils, I realized it smelled a bit like that black stuff that had been on my hands. A little like tar and rotten eggs, except not nearly as strong and unpleasant. I'm not sure why it wasn't as sharp and stinky as the black stuff had been with that same combination, but it wasn't. Maybe because there was also something else mixed in with the faint tar-sulfur smell. Something almost flowery. The combination was both soothing and weirdly pleasant. The sort of smell that made me want to smile, same as I did when filing my lungs with pine-scented forest air.

Given my reaction to the black stuff, the fact that I found the baby's scent nice struck me as… significant in a way I couldn't quite describe. My logical brain was trying to find a way to disprove what my instinctive brain was telling it about the baby. About the baby being *not* a lizard, at least not an ordinary lizard. About the rocks and boulders that looked like a dragon being *not* just rocks and boulders.

Real life dictated that the rocks were just rocks. And the thing curled up on my stomach was just a lizard.

But I knew better.

As we watched the rain slowly stopped, until all that was left were drips and plinks from the leaves to the brown soil. The warmth from the dragon rocks eased and the cave got cool again. Not quite cold. But that could have been because I had a baby sitting warmly on my stomach. The rocks beneath my back were definitely cooler now, though.

"Okay, little one," I said to the baby as I started to ease up into a sitting position. "That's my cue to leave. I need to get home." I gave its head another pet, cupping my hand around under its chin to scratch along its jaws. It seemed to like that. I smiled. "Thanks for not cooking me or eating me. I hope something that is food comes along soon."

The baby made that cooing noise, and when I tried to lift it off me, a slight hiss. I settled it again and met its gaze. "I need to leave. I can't live in a cave. I have a house. That's where humans like me live. I have a husband—that's a life partner. Do your species do that?" I glanced at the rocks. "Probably not, huh. Well, he's someone I spend a lot of time with. And he'd miss me if I stayed here. So I need to go home."

The baby made a sad little hissing sound and climbed off me, easing back as I stood. I kept my movements slow and careful. Then I went around the rocky tail I'd hopped over earlier and retrieved my backpack, glad to see it hadn't been singed when the baby had shot off that rush of fire. The baby had followed and nuzzled the pack as I picked it up, so I squatted down and showed them what was inside.

"Just my hiking supplies," I said, "though I should have brought a raincoat, right?"

It half climbed into the bag and came out with one of my protein bars in its mouth.

"Oh, wait! Let me take the wrapper off. I'm not sure what that might do to your digestive system." I unwrapped the chocolate and granola bar and then handed it back to the baby who took it delicately from my hand. Given its mouth full of teeth, I appreciated its consideration in not snapping off one of my fingers in its hurry.

It slurped down the bar. I'm not even sure if it chewed or not. Then its little eyes widened and it nudged my bag again.

"Sorry," I said. "That was my last one."

I stood, using the rocks that looked like a tail to balance and wasn't surprised the stone was cold now. Or at least I pretended not to be surprised. Part of me was yelling that none of this made sense. A louder part was telling me I was encountering something extraordinary and to not question it too much.

"It was nice to meet you," I said to the baby. "Truly. This is definitely something I'll never forget."

The baby followed me as I walked to the cave mouth. And when I started out, heading back down the trail that would wind its way to my car, the baby called out in its little cooing-hiss.

I smiled at it and waved. "Thanks for keeping me warm. Good luck!"

Chapter Three

It will probably come as no surprise that by the time I got back to my house the baby was waiting on a corner of the roof, near the gutter, its tail wrapped around its body, its wings tucked tightly to its sides. It coo-hissed when it saw me and leapt off the roof into my arms, almost knocking us over again.

I'm not entirely sure how it found my house before I even got there. I thought maybe it followed my scent, but if that was the case, its sense of smell was outrageously good. It probably could have also flown over my car all the way back. Either way, when I asked, it didn't bother to explain.

My husband took the new "pet" in stride. He's pretty easy going that way. He loves animals, especially cats. And Baby was quite a bit like a cat.

Just without the fur. And with the occasional habit of breathing fire when really ticked off.

We had to be careful, of course, and it took a lot of reading to figure out exactly how to take care of Baby. The first trip to the vet was a lesson for sure. Trying to pass off a baby dragon as a lizard with someone trained to know what lizards were had been ridiculous. But for reasons that were not discussed openly, after a brief pause and an assessing look, the vet carried on with the exam and ensured Baby was healthy. She gave me a couple of pamphlets with instructions for taking care of baby "lizards"—the word "lizards" was in quotes on the pamphlets—and advised me to bring Baby in annual for a checkup.

Our neighborhood remained pest free after that, though it did take some discussions to explain to Baby what was and wasn't "food" first. Dogs and cats and birds—not food. Rats and mice and anything Baby found in the mountains that didn't belong to a human—could work as food. Once that was sorted, none of the neighbors complained. None of them acknowledged that Baby was more than a lizard either.

No one ever talked about it out loud. About the fact that those rocks that looked like a dragon in the cave across the valley were more than rocks. No one ever mentioned that our new pet "lizard" wasn't a lizard, even though it had wings and could fly and breathed fire occasionally. Baby was just Baby. There were the occasional winks and nudges, knowing *looks* exchanged with Baby's vet. But that was it.

Apparently, according to the pamphlets, that was just the way the dragon redistribution system worked.

Who was I to argue?

Dragons of Some Kind

Chapter One

Tanith stood at the edge of the river, tossing in small rocks, trying to make them skip, wondering if she could get a good solid two jumps out of a rock that wasn't right for skipping. Something about the challenge of skipping a "bad" rock, the kind her older brother would have determined unskippable back in the day, drove Tanith to try.

Not that she was having much luck. Her mind wasn't really in it. Skipping rocks was a distraction. A way to stop thinking. Thinking in that moment was her enemy.

And she had a lot of enemies crowding against the door of her mind.

Later, she promised herself. She'd think about it all later.

She skipped another odd shaped, too-spherical rock. Or tried to. It went one bounce and then sank deep into the fast-moving river water. The banks were surrounded by aspen and pine, the mix of white trunks, yellowing leaves, and green pine needles sparkling on the clear river water. The air was fresh, an earlier rain leaving behind cooler temperatures and a real fall taste in the air. She had never been sure how to explain that to her brother. That fall had a taste. But it did. A little thinner than summer air, but not as sharp and apple-crisp like winter. There was still a mild crispness to it, though. More like spices. And maybe a bit of a honey sweetness.

Yeah, hard to explain. She didn't have the words exactly. Her brother had always said there was a different *look* to fall, a change in the kind and quality of light. He explained it as like someone had wiped a window clean, so the air was clearer, but also there was a softness to it.

She couldn't quite see what he did, and he couldn't quite taste what she did, but the sentiment was the same. Fall was unique. And for Tanith, the best time of the year. Usually.

But this year, she had a problem. Even the rolling, rapid waters of the river, the bubbling clear currents rushing over rocks, creating pocket eddies full of sticks and dead leaves, couldn't hold off her problem for long.

She skipped another stone. A good one this time. Flat and round and just the sort her brother would approve of. Much to her irritation, she got a good solid five jumps from it before it sank beneath the water.

Hamish would gloat. Good thing he wasn't around to see.

The crack of a dried stick behind her straightened her spine. Already? She wasn't quite ready for this confrontation yet. But hiding from her thoughts wasn't the only thing that had brought her to the river.

She turned slowly, not wanting to startle them. They'd come at her request, but that didn't mean they wouldn't disappear as soon as she faced them. The rocky bank underfoot shifted and sent rocks skittering around as she moved, creating a backdrop crinkling sound to the rolling river water.

Despite taking a fortifying breath, knowing what she was here for, she still paused when she finally faced them and had to give herself some time to adjust.

They weren't…ugly really. But also not majestic and beautiful the way one might expect. Probably because they were so old. Hamish said they were dragons of some kind, but she wasn't sure she'd have described them that way if she didn't know what they were.

Three of them. On spindly legs that didn't seem to have joints for bending, though the legs were close enough to the ground, and numbered in the hundreds, so maybe they didn't need to bend. Their bodies were long and serpentine. Not covered in scales, though. Those snake-like bodies were actually covered in feathers. Sharp, brown and gray, ragged looking feathers. Like a molting chick who'd never finished molting. Patches of pale pink skin shone through areas where the molting feathers had left gaps. In other areas, the brown and gray feathers were fluffed up enough to almost look healthy.

All three had long, wedge shaped heads, though the one in the middle's head was longer in the nose than the other two. They had raised nostrils at the end of those snouts. And forked tongues danced out to taste the air. Long and black, covered in small nubs of taste cells. She absently wondered if fall tasted the same to them as it did to her.

They were each about the length of a large school bus, so she couldn't really see their tail tips as she was more focused on their heads. Her brother had described the tails as tipped with a spike-like needle they could use like a bee stinger, but didn't often because it sapped their strength and they had to spend time regrowing that stinger.

Still, she wouldn't want to encounter the wrong end of those needle-thin spikes so she kept her hands folded in front of her and her gaze turned down even as she kept all three in her sights.

They had eyes. But the eyes were large, and black, and impossible to read. A sort of combination of bird and snake. Liquid clear lids flickered over their eyes, leaving a glossy shine. And she knew from Hamish that though the eyes looked solid, there were actually a multitude of facets that caught many images at once.

The mere thought of that kind of view gave her a headache.

She dipped her head in greeting and said, "Thank you, ancient ones, for answering my plea."

"Why have you called us?" The sibilant sound of all three voices combined into one still managed to echo in the open clearing beside the river.

She didn't see their mouths moving. Their tongues continued to taste the air. She wasn't sure how they were talking, and talking with one voice—she could hear the three distinct tones in that voice, but it still sounded as if only one of them was speaking—but they could communicate this way with her, and that was a relief. Hamish hadn't been sure, and she wasn't very good at communicating in other ways yet.

"My brother. He needs...help."

"He should have petitioned himself."

"I know. He knows. But… You see, he couldn't come. The…the quickening has begun. He's afraid to leave the house. It's too soon. And we live among people who would not understand."

"Hamish…"

The way the three said her brother's name—that they *knew* his name without her telling them—made her shiver.

"He has not provided tribute. Are you the tribute?"

"No." This part he was clear on. She was not to give them a tribute of any kind. He didn't explain why, though, which made negotiation much more difficult. "He petitions in earnest, but will give no tribute."

"Without tribute, there can be no aid. He has brought this on himself."

The three started backward, their jointless stumps of legs moving against the rocks, making them shift and crinkle. Their long bodies undulating in reverse.

"Wait!" She couldn't let them go. Hamish needed help. This was his only chance. "Wait. Please. He's desperate. I'm desperate. Please."

"There is no help without payment. A tribute."

"I…don't understand the tribute. Please. Explain. Maybe we can…come to an arrangement."

Her brother would be angry she'd even left open the possibility, but since he hadn't told her what it meant, what the consequences of the tribute were, how could she not ask. Especially when the three were about to leave.

"Tribute…" They edged forward again. "The sacrifice must be made. Consequences are required."

"Consequences for what?" Hamish hadn't done anything wrong. He'd taken care of her her whole life, ensured they were safe, housed, fed. He kept them from suspicious gazes and made sure they could live comfortably without fear. As far as she knew, he'd never done anything that merited negative consequences. In fact, he'd already done so much sacrificing, to ensure her life was safe, she felt he'd more than paid in that.

The three eased forward, the one in the center moving beyond the others to get close enough its forked tongue could reach Tanith. It tasted the air around her, not actually touching her with the sensitive tips, but the vibrating motion of it tasting her scent created a sort of rattling noise against the rushing river and crinkling rocks.

This close, she finally got their flavor too. Musty, with a slight sting to the edge of it. There was a sweetness too but an old and foul sort of sweetness. Like detritus rotting in a jungle. And under all that, a bitter taste of rancid eggs. Fortunately for her stomach, the rancid egg flavor was faint. She had to concentrate to taste it. So she didn't concentrate, just let the flavors enter into her subconscious without stopping too long to consider them.

The central creature snapped its black tongue back into its mouth. "Hamish stole an egg."

"An egg?"

"Long ago. He should have not stolen the egg. Now, he will quicken too fast. It will destroy him. He must ensure the tribute is paid, or there is nothing we can do."

None of this made sense to her. Hamish had always been cagey about their ancestry, but he'd told her some of it. Obviously not enough. "If I retrieve the egg, is that the tribute you require?"

"It is the only acceptable tribute. Without it, the quickening will kill him."

Shit. No. She couldn't lose him. They were all they'd ever had. She wouldn't know how to continue on in this world without him.

"What does this egg look like?" She'd never seen a strange egg among their belongings, so she had to assume it didn't look like a standard chicken egg or even something the size of an ostrich. It was a treasure, obviously, since they were upset that Hamish had supposedly stolen it. Perhaps it was more of a jewel? Like a Fabergé egg or something like that?

"For that, you must ask Hamish."

"No, wait." She held up a hand, afraid they'd leave. "Why is this egg important? What am I looking for? Please, I don't understand any of this. I just know Hamish needs help."

The creature who'd tasted her scent moved even closer. So close, their noses practically touched. It looked at her from those fathomless black eyes, perched forward on its wedge head, and Tanith couldn't look away.

She felt herself falling, tumbling. And then the water closed over her head as she sank down into blackness…

Chapter Two

Everything was dark. Dank. A faint clinking of water dripping from rock. She could feel the rocks, the depth, the warmth and humidity. A shiver went through her, even though the air was warm. Not because of the temperature. Fear trembled along her skin, raising goosebumps.

Tanith couldn't see. But the taste of her surroundings sparked dread and she wasn't sure why. The top layers were flavored with minerals, and warmth, and a touch of silver. There was a crispness of bitter heat, like the depths of summer. A bite of acid. And that hint of foul eggs there beneath it all.

This wasn't a scent she remembered and yet it seemed imprinted on her. The scent of fear. The scent of something…happening.

Sounds only slow rose to her awareness. Sounds like sharp metal moving over rock. Sounds like grunting and grinding. The grinding of something hard that needed to be broken down. Scraping. Breaking. Dissolving.

And then a new taste filled the air. Powdery flakes of something like…like honey? No. More like slivers of almond. And also shimmery cold like snow. This was a flavor she'd never encountered before. Harder to describe than even attempting to tell Hamish what fall tasted like. There was more than the snow and almond flavors. Depths of textures that defied her vocabulary. Completely different to anything she'd encountered. There was something like blood there, and dust, and… sweetness but mixed with a bitter bite that almost hurt. None of the foul egg scent, though. In fact, this new smell completely overpowered the smell of wherever she was.

And it lit up inside her like a beacon of…hope?

How odd.

More metal moving over rock, the scraping noise making her skin crawl, making her ears hurt. A spark in the darkness. Too bright for eyes grown used to seeing only blackness. She winced and narrowed her gaze until her eyes adjusted.

Still all she could see were shadows against the light, shadows moving on a stone wall. The shadows of a human, bending, picking something up and cradling it close. Leaving behind something else. A bundle of some kind. The scents that sparked hope seemed centered in that bundle, whatever it was. Surrounding the human-shaped person, but also inside the bundle.

Tanith tried to get closer but couldn't seem to move.

A memory, she realized. Or a vision? But some of this felt oddly familiar, though she'd never been here before.

The bundle. She wanted to see what was inside the bundle.

There was some scraping metal again. The rocks beneath her rumbled, sending a warning vibration up her legs. The surroundings filled with a hissing sound.

"Your tribute is acceptable," a quiet voice echoed against stone walls that dripped with dampness. "But how will you raise her?"

"That's my business," a second voice said. It didn't seem to be coming from the human holding whatever they were holding in exchange for the bundle that tasted like hope. "We are done. Satisfied with the exchange."

"We are…sssatisfied. For now."

"No. Not for now. There will be no more. This is

the tribute. If you cannot accept it, tell me now. I'll take it back."

"No!"

A sudden movement and something Tanith couldn't quite see flowed around the bundle. Shadow but solid, with a hint of something sharp in the lines—spikes maybe. She couldn't be sure when all she could see were shadows moving against the stone wall.

"The quickening will come," the first voice said as it slithered around the offering. "You cannot hold it off forever."

"This will help. This is the focus I need."

"And when it fails?"

"Then I will know you've betrayed your promise."

"I promised her in exchange for this." More movement around the bundle. "I make no promises that this will work."

"It will work."

The darkness closed in suddenly, cutting off the shadow tableau.

And Tanith found herself sinking into the depths of the water again.

A NEW FLAVOR COATED HER TONGUE, THE TASTE OF home. Familiar in its textures. Hamish and their cat Marie-Beth. The flavors of spice and meat from the last meals prepared together as Hamish taught her to cook—she was indifferent to the process but she liked to eat so she forced herself to learn enough to get by. There was the taste of fresh soap from the laundry room, old sweat baked into the walls carrying the flavors of those she loved best, clean cat litter, the sharp sting of cleaning fluid where they'd had to clean up after the bird Marie-Beth had brought into the house, the tang of clean clothes and modern electronics.

Home.

Something tightened in Tanith's chest. Left her breathless. This was where Hamish was, hurting, struggling, desperate for answers. And she had none for him. Only this visions, this journey the three had sent her on. But she didn't understand any of it. Even the familiar parts.

"You have to let me help." A voice. Her voice. Down the hall. She blinked and looked around. She was in the living room. But the voice had come from the hallway outside their bedrooms.

"There is no help." Hamish, but his voice deep with strain. With the pain of the quickening. "They will not do more now. Not without…giving them more than I'm willing to give."

"What? What can't you give? Maybe I can? This isn't right. It's too soon."

"No! No tributes. Do not give them a tribute, do you hear me? Enough was given. They will twist the terms. It can't help."

"They'll have the answers. I have to ask. I have to try."

Harsh breath. Teeth grinding together so hard she winced. A low moan he'd tried to keep to himself and failed. More harsh breathing. Then, sounding even more strained, "You can try. They won't help. But don't let them talk you into a tribute. Enough has been paid."

TANITH BLINKED AND LOOKED AROUND, THE CHANGE this time so sudden she hadn't even experienced the falling, drowning sensation. Back in the darkness but with a faint glow, like fire, to reveal the cavern. The dripping walls caught the light from the glow and sparkled like stars imbedded in night sky. Something slid past her leg and she gasped, jumping to one side so fast her shoulder bumped against rock. The jolt sent a pain down her arm, to her fingers, making her nerves tingle.

Her tongue stung with a bitterness in the air, acrid and burning. The taste was so strong it coated her mouth and made her want to gag. Her nose stung.

A ruffling of something like feathers. The scrape of metal over rock. "I must have more. I must have more. It was not enough." The voice from the first vision, the one who'd spoken to the human. When the offering was made.

"It is never enough." This a deeper voice Tanith hadn't heard before.

"I must have more," the first voice. Higher. Discordant as it resonated through the rocks, creating an almost feedback loop of harsh sensation in Tanith's bones. "He will quicken. He will quicken without giving me more."

"There was never any promise he would not."

"I must have more!"

"There can be no more. Not without a new egg. A new tribute."

A screaming wail that pierced Tanith's ears. She covered them against the sound as it bounced around the walls, getting louder and harsher rather than fading away. The scream brought Tanith to her knees, stole her breath. Hit a primordial fear that made her want to scream back, to demand the terrible noise stop. To give the screamer whatever they wanted if they would only stop the horrible wail.

The sound cut off suddenly. So suddenly Tanith's ears rang with it.

And silence and blackness descended again.

Chapter Three

Tanith floated in a pool of liquid quiet and cool darkness. No heat here to taste. No bitter, sharp flavors. Sweet fresh things like parsley and basil. A hint of crispness. Cucumber this time. Lots of rich undertones that shivered over her and left her content and at ease.

She couldn't remember ever feeling quite this way. Maybe in those childhood days, skipping rocks with Hamish across ponds and rivers. Once at a lake big enough for them to fish in. This was even more peaceful than that, though. Almost like death. No more things to worry about. No more pain or fear.

Had she died? She didn't think so. She felt the water lapping her skin. Warm and soothing, like a bath. She felt the air above her swirling in gentle currents. There were too many flavors in the air. It was all to…substantial for death.

Where was she this time?

"Home," a voice in the dark whispered. It sounded like her own voice. None of the ones she'd heard up to now. But she didn't trust it.

"This isn't my home. My home is with Hamish."

"Are you sure?"

"Yes."

"He will destroy you after the quickening."

"I'm here to stop that, to stop his quickening. I don't want him to die."

"He could die if he hurts you. And he *will* hurt you."

"There has to be a way. A way to stop the quickening. He was sure there would be."

"He came for that answer once. We warned him it would fail."

"What answer did you give him?"

"He believed rescuing one of the younglings would stall his quickening. Would push it off so that he could raise the youngling. He thought, like his mother before him, that he could delay until he was ready for the change. His are cursed to quicken too fast, and destroy before they settle. If they survive. His quickening began too soon. He will not survive it. But raising a youngling can only put off the change for so long. Not as long as he needs."

She floated silently for a timeless moment, aware time must pass but not feeling it. "Was I the youngling?"

"You were. Your kind eat their young if the young cannot escape. It is why there are so few of you. Hamish found a tribute. He sped your hatching, then gave your dam a mixture of the remains—shell, sac, all that was left—prepared in a very special way to satisfy the craving. And satisfy it did. Too well. Your dam wishes more tribute."

"We can't give her more. There is no more shell."

"There is you."

"If I die, it will save Hamish?"

"No. He is…too attached to his sister now. A sister he raised from infancy. You have memories of parents?"

"I do." She had memories of them losing their parents when she was only three or four years old—young enough to not really remember them—and Hamish stepping up to raise her because he was older.

"Using his gifts did not help his cause. He shortened the time to the quickening with each working."

"Magic?" Hamish had never admitted to such. But his kind were not unknown to have gifts.

Until this floating pool of darkness, she'd

assumed she was of the same kind. Though no magical gifts had ever arisen for her.

It only occurred to her, after another quiet moment of water lapping against her skin, that her kind were…not what she'd thought.

"I will eat my young?"

"You will crave the eggs, should you choose to produce any. It might be better if you did not. You have been human for a long time. It would not sit well with you after."

The voice was right. That wouldn't sit well with her. But that was a problem for another day. A decision that could be made at any time. She was here to save her brother.

Something there, though. "He delayed his quickening with me, by having a youngling to raise. He could delay it again with a new youngling. Will any kind of dragon do?"

Silence settled into the darkness. Long enough, she thought she might have been abandoned to her questions with no more answers to be found here. But the setting didn't change again. Nothing changed. She floated. Tasting the sweet, fresh, herby flavors of the air. The warm water gentle against her skin. Tears leaked down her temple into the pool. She hadn't realized she was crying until the long quiet. She wanted to raise her hand to wipe the tears away but when she tried, her limbs didn't move.

Normally, that might have panicked her, but here, there didn't seem to be room for panic.

After what could have been moments or years, the voice returned. "A new youngling would forestall his quickening again. Perhaps long enough for him to be ready. But only a youngling of your kind will do. And there are none at present. Your dam craves more of the tribute. She might be persuaded to create another egg. But she will have a hard time not eating it too soon. And Hamish must prepare the tribute. His kind are the only ones who can."

The voice paused. Then, "If you ask your dam for a new egg, with the promise of more tribute, she might listen. But she might also consume you in her quest for the flavor she craves. She might not have the patience anymore to wait. Unfortunately, the tribute Hamish provided was…too much more, and it has created an unnatural craving for her. Going to her will likely only end in your death."

That was why Hamish told her not to offer another tribute. That was why she wasn't to exchange anything.

Everything made more sense now. Parts of her life she'd questioned, but had ignored getting answers to those questions for fear it might hurt her brother somehow. His protectiveness and vague details about their parents. The way she'd never developed the skills he had, but was seeing different skills in herself. Things she hadn't talked to him about. Assumed they were just part of growing up.

But she couldn't look to Hamish for answers for her own quickening. She was a different kind.

A different kind of dragon.

"Can I produce a youngling that will delay Hamish's quickening? Could my hatchling do for him what I did for him?"

"You will demand tribute and crave the egg. You cannot delay his quickening with offspring of your own without risking what there is of your humanity to produce the egg."

"Will my quickening kill me?"

"No. That is not the way of your kind."

"So the only problem is that I might destroy any egg I produce?"

"That is the thing Hamish fears. It is why he doesn't explain."

"Would my dam come for me, if I produced an egg? Would she attempt to steal my egg for herself?"

"It is also a potential problem. But her craving is for…more now. Your flavors. Not your offspring. She is more dangerous to you than to any you create. To those you create, you are the dangerous one."

They needed a sibling. Someone for Hamish to

raise so that he could delay his transformation longer. Until he was ready and could do so without dying. But if she tried to produce an egg—and she was not ready for that yet, she was sure; it might not even be possible yet—they risk her losing her hold on what made her Tanith. If she went to her dam, she risked her dam simply eating her.

She didn't want to produce an egg under these circumstances, risk losing herself and never being able to save Hamish. He'd raised her, protected her…taught her to skip rocks. She'd do anything to keep him from dying.

But part of that had to be keeping herself too. For his sake as well as hers.

She thought about the fact that he'd taken her in simply to forestall his own quickening, that the initial adoption had nothing to do with her as an individual and everything to do with him. Yet, in the end, they were family and he had raised her well. Even given her the idea of parents so she'd feel loved and comforted. She would have died, eaten by her real dam, if not for Hamish. However their family was started, they were family now, well and truly.

And he would not want her to sacrifice who she was for him. He'd made that very clear.

"I will speak with my dam. She craves the tribute. We can come to an arrangement."

"Your brother will object. He does not wish you to provide more tribute."

"He thinks my dam will kill me."

"She may."

"It's a risk I can take."

"You will not risk producing your own egg?"

"Not now. Maybe not ever. But that's a consideration for later. Or a last resort. I'm hoping we don't need it."

"Then your decision is made."

"It is."

Her body jerked downward, the water covered her face, and she sank to the depths…

Chapter Four

Tanith blinked hard against the glare surrounding her, only slowly taking in the tastes on the air. Fall crisp and clean. The river bubbling and rumbling behind her. The crinkling of current over stone. The three musty-feathered dragons before her.

When her eyes adjusted, Tanith looked up at the three. They were all standing several yards away now, watching her closely with their black eyes. The feathers along their serpentine bodies ruffled as a gentle breeze blew past.

"You will go to your dam. Despite what your brother wishes."

"It's the only way?"

"It's the only way. If you do not wish to produce an egg of your own."

That, she realized as she stared up at the three, was the real reason Hamish had told her not to offer tribute. They would tell her to produce an egg. And she wasn't ready. She wouldn't have known she'd crave it, eat it before it could hatch. He hadn't told her that part of her nature. Maybe he'd been afraid of hurting her, telling her this about her kind of dragons. It hardly mattered now. He'd kept that information from her. And she realized he'd done it because he'd feared she'd sacrifice her own peace of mind, her own soul, to save him.

He was right in some ways. She would do much to save him. And the thing she would do was the one thing none of them thought she'd do.

She'd face her dam.

"She will try to destroy you," the center dragon said. "It is her nature to eat that which she creates."

"I'm no longer hers. She hasn't had a hand in *creating* me since I was hatched. Eating me would no longer satisfy her craving." Tanith was sure of this, though she wasn't sure how.

Perhaps more knowledge had been settled in her mind than just the explanations the voice in the dark pool had given her. Or perhaps these were instincts that went deeper. Either way, in the bright fall sunlight at the edge of the river, she knew she was no longer her dam's creation. And therefore, her dam would no longer crave her.

She might kill Tanith still, for the audacity to speak to her. But she wouldn't crave her.

"Where do I find her?"

"Ah, that is the easy part." The three dragons wove together, moving in a way that was hard to follow, their jointless bottom limbs clacking against the rocks. "We can take you there."

She gasped quietly when all three seemed to weave into one. A braid of serpent bodies covered in feathers that no longer looked scruffy and dirty. Silver spread across the feathers, and wings that hadn't been part of any of the individuals spread out from the sides of the woven body. The hundreds of jointless legs pulled up inside the body, the dragons now resting on the ground like a snake.

"You will have to risk a ride with us to gain her audience." All three said at once, in that combined voice of theirs. "It is how Hamish made his journey for you. Will you risk this fate?"

"For my brother?" She crossed to them without hesitating. "Yes."

Chapter Five

The flight was high, well above the range that risked anyone observing them. The ground beneath fell away sharply, and a fog of cool clouds surrounded them as they moved forward, obscuring them from view, but also hiding the landscape below. Tanith had no idea where they flew to and wouldn't have been able to find the location of her dam again without this ride. She suspected that was the point.

The air up this high tasted like fresh water, ice crystals, clean and brisk. A rainy kind of flavor, though the clouds also held hints of minerals and acid, flavors that hit bitter against her tongue. There was no trail to the tastes, though. Nothing increasing or decreasing that she'd have been able to use to track their journey.

And she was sure that was the point as well.

When they finally started to descend, the clouds around them broke to reveal a harsh, rocky mountain range covered in black rocks and low, scrubby bushes. No trees or forest here. But not barren either. The foliage was dark. Brown and rust colored. Snow covered the top third of the range. And the air above this place tasted of ancient minerals and bitter roots.

The three angled down into a valley between two of the larger mountains in the range. And here, some actual greenery. The valley below was covered in mats of soft grass. A thin river ran down the center. And here and there, a tree taller than her with green needles covering its branches.

The black rock walls of the valley had several large caves opening into them. She wondered if they were going to one of those caves. But no, the three didn't fly there. They instead circled down to a grassy bank near this new river.

From the visions she'd had earlier, she expected darkness and dank. Not the taste of wet grass and rich damp soil. The flavor of snow carried down into the valley since the river water had originated in the snowy mountain peaks. The air was cool, a cold breeze blowing through the grass. She was already chilled from the ride in the clouds and the cold air cooled her more. That was nice. She hated being too hot.

Feet on the spongy grass, she glanced up and down the valley, wondering which way her dam would approach. She'd thought this place might feel vaguely familiar. It was, after all, the place she'd been hatched. But there was nothing on this grassy bank, not even the flavors, that felt familiar. Unlike the dark pool in her vision. Unlike the cavern where she'd seen the shadows of her dam and Hamish negotiating for her. Those had tasted like somewhere she might have been before. This place did not.

"It is neutral ground for your meeting," the three said in unison. "She would not have you in her cavern. The scent would drive her to a rage."

"Why? Because she didn't get to eat me?"

"Because now that you are alive, you are a rival. One day, you will quicken. And you will have eggs of your own. Even if you have chosen not to rush that process right now, it will happen. Eventually. And you will be a rival for this world."

"If I never produce eggs or move past the initial stages of the quickening, will I still be a rival to her?"

"You will always be a threat. The cravings are not the only reason your kind eat their eggs."

"Why lay them then, if we just devour them or view any survivors as a threat?"

"The instincts to perpetuate oneself are nearly as strong as the craving."

"The biology of our kind is weird." And she meant it. She might be a dragon of some kind but she had never understood the different aspects of dragon biology. And outside of helping Hamish, she wasn't sure she wanted to know. She preferred her life as it was now.

"All biology is weird," the three said. "From a certain point of view."

She supposed that was true. She flexed her toes inside her tennis shoes, half wanting to take them off and walk on the soft grass in her bare feet. But there wasn't time for that.

Or maybe there was. Her dam kept them waiting. Tanith had no idea how long. She wasn't wearing a watch and didn't have her phone with her for this quest. Time meant very little to most dragons. No matter the species. They lived long and moved slowly unless they chose to move fast. But a fast-moving dragon tended to be the last thing seen by the being in the way of that fast-moving dragon.

She was a little impatient, because she was afraid, and because Hamish was in trouble and needed this. But she was also content to draw out the wait. Until the wait ended, she had no answers and still had hope her dam would negotiate with her. She could only hold on to that hope so long as she was waiting.

The three separated and settled into the cool grass as well, each curling into separate coils, their jointless legs remaining retracted inside their bodies. Settled in to wait just like her.

At the edge of the river, she found some stones and began skipping them over the water, deeper and faster here than the river where she'd found the three. Most of the stones she picked up were too jagged, but she occupied her time trying to get more than one skip out of them. She managed four skips of one almost perfectly shaped rock before it sank beneath the deep blue water.

When she turned back from that triumph to find another rock, she spotted the eyes watching her from several yards away, peeking around a one of the few pine trees scattered along the valley floor. The eyes were large. And orangish red. Like the rust colors of the higher altitudes in this place.

Tanith froze in place, holding the gaze of those huge orange eyes.

"You have come to my territory," a high voice slithered out from behind the tree. "Why? To bring me a snack?"

"To negotiate. For my brother."

"He brought me the best tribute." The words

purred out, followed by a clicking and the raw sound of metal scraping over rock. "I will negotiate for that tribute."

"He needs another egg for that tribute. We cannot make it without the shell."

"And the youngling? They will be part of the tribute?"

"The tribute would not be the same with the youngling. It will never taste the same, be the same, with the youngling. The youngling must be given to us, so that the tribute will meet the memory of the last."

"I would eat the youngling as well. A snack for my tribute."

"There will be no tribute if the youngling is consumed." Talking about this, about eating a youngling, made Tanith's stomach turn. Knowing this was her lot, that her dragon would crave such things after the quicken, sickened her. But she kept those emotions buried because her dam would smell them.

"You assume I will do this as a favor for you? Because you are my child? I know why you want the youngling. To extend your brother's time before his quickening." The dragon moved out from behind the tree, just her upper body, but it was enough.

She was large, but not as large as the three. A dragon made of silver scales so bright and shiny they looked like polished metal. There were lines of mineral deposits along the edges of her scales, winking with purple and gold light. She tasted of those minerals, and metal, and that tang of heat. This kind of dragon breathed fire from its long snout, and even now those raised nostrils puffed smoke. There was a distinct taste of foul egg around the dragon, but that was beneath the heavier flavors of melting metal. The flavor made Tanith's tongue tingle.

And created a strange sort of hunger in her.

"You wish to save a dragon of another kind," her dam said. "Because he saved you? But only for selfish reasons."

"Yes. And I will repay him for that. For selfish reasons."

"Whhhyyy? Because he will taste good when you eat him?"

Tanith couldn't help her wince. Why did she have to come from such a species. "No. Because he's my brother. And I don't want to lose him. He'll die if he quickens now. It's still too soon."

"You extended that time already."

"And you know another youngling will give him more time."

"I'd rather eat the youngling than see another of mine prosper only to come asking for favors." She slithered forward farther. There were legs beneath the long, thick body, but they were short and out to the side of her torso, like an allegator, half hidden in the grass. With her legs hidden that way, she almost looked like a giant snake. "Or maybe," she said, on a quiet hiss, "maybe you two will come to destroy me. Why should I risk such traitorous behavior?"

"For the tribute," Tanith said. There was no point making promises that she or another of her dam's offspring wouldn't return to kill their dam. There were no guarantees in life and Tanith had no idea what kind of dragon she'd really be in the end. Her dam would see through false promises. So she didn't bother. She went right to the heart of the matter.

The thing she knew her dam craved above all else. She'd said as much in that vision.

"I can eat you as tribute."

"I won't give you the same high. I won't satisfy that craving that has left you sleepless and desperate. But with an egg, we can hatch it and create the tribute you want."

"And if I don't agree?"

"You will never again taste that flavor." Tanith shrugged. "The choice is yours."

Another long pause as her dam flowed a few more feet forward. The sound of metal scrapping over rock. Her tongue flickered out, a fast, sharp movement. Unlike the three, her tongue was not forked and was pink instead of black. But Tanith had no doubt she tasted as much on the air as the three. Or even as Tanith. Maybe more. There was always more after the quickening.

"Your brother will agree to this?"

"He will." He'd have no choice once she brought him an egg. She was already doing the thing he hadn't wanted her to do. No going back now.

"If he fails to provide my tribute, after I have held up my part of the bargain, it will not go well for either of you."

"We'll uphold our part of the bargain. One egg. And you receive your tribute."

Her dam wanted that flavor too much to resist. Tanith could see it, *taste* it in the air. The longing and desperation, with flavors like brittle tar and musk. Her dam's rust-colored eyes widened, inner, transparent lids winked down, making her look like she'd blinked.

"One egg," her dam said. "And I will receive my tribute."

A person walked out from behind the silver dragon, carrying something large in a leather rucksack. Tanith held very still. But she frowned because she hadn't tasted another person here. Hadn't been aware that someone was with her dam. And that felt like a very dangerous failure. She pulled in a breath and tried to parse out his flavor separate from her dam. But all she tasted was her dam. The man, clearly a man now that he stood next to the silver dragon's head, seemed to have no flavor but that of the dragon.

Was he her offspring too? But no, Tanith's own flavors weren't a match to her dam. Or to Hamish for that matter. Hers were unique. Everyone she'd encountered so far has a unique scent, a personal flavor. Either this man did not, or his and the silver dragon's flavors were so intertwined she couldn't pull them apart.

"We wondered if you'd come," the man said. His voice was deep. The voice in the vision, speaking with her dam.

Tanith blinked. She'd been expecting that one to be a dragon of some kind, too.

Maybe he was. Maybe he hadn't quickened yet.

"I am a dragon," he said, as if reading her thoughts. "A different kind than any you might have encountered before. But I fear we have little time for explanations." He held up the rucksack. "We thought you might petition for a new egg. I've kept her from eating this one as long as I can. Had you arrived any later, we would have no ready egg to make this exchange. The previous three were not so lucky. But, as you can tell, she is eager for Hamish's tribute again. So we've been preparing."

Tanith stared at the rucksack. From the outside,

it was just a simple brown leather bag with a flap over the top to seal it shut. No zips, just a button through a leather loop to hold that top down. The bag looked old and worn. Well used. Whatever was inside was probably the size of a basketball. Maybe a little larger. But smaller than one might assume a dragon egg would be.

She'd never seen a dragon egg in person before. Heard and read things, of course. But she and Hamish kept away from most of the kinds. Content to live as humans in the human world. A world they both wished to live in for a little while longer.

"How long until it hatches?" she asked.

The man said, "It will hatch on its own in another month, but is close enough for Hamish to speed the hatching without harm. She must have the tribute within the week or she will come looking for you."

Her dam clicked her teeth together and her body moved so that the sound of metal on rocks was an ominous punctuation to the man's final sentence.

"This will be the last tribute," Tanith said.

Though even as the words left her, she wondered. Now that she knew her siblings, the offspring of her dam, would mostly be devoured before even hatching, she considered that maybe, for the sake of the offspring themselves, maybe this wouldn't be the last tribute. But making that promise, saying that out loud felt like a step too far and would lead to trouble for her and Hamish. So she didn't take back her statement. But in the back of her head, she left open the possibility.

Her dam's orange eyes flickered with the blinking of her translucent inner lids. Her only response to Tanith's statement.

The man said, "You know how to find us, should you change your mind."

After a brief glance at the silver dragon, he passed the leather rucksack to Tanith. "The egg is comfortably cushioned inside. I'd recommend not opening that until you get home."

"What if you've given me something that isn't an egg?"

He shrugged and flicked open the buttoned closure on the sack's top flap, then lifted the flap.

Inside the rucksack, a cushion of cloth scraps surrounded an egg the size of an ostrich egg. Not nearly as large as Tanith had assumed it would be, given it would birth a dragon of some kind. The weight of the bag was heavy in her hands too, requiring her to use both arms to hold it safely and not risk dropping it. Yet the egg itself looked delicate, weightless. The outer shell was a purplish color circled by a pattern in gold that was almost like scales, but so faint it could have just been marbling. There was a thicker patch of gold-colored leather at the top of the egg, and she wondered if there would be a matching at the base, or was this the only cap.

The pictures she'd seen of various eggs didn't quite do them justice. At least not her dam's egg. This one was shimmery and beautiful. Almost like a Fabergé egg with only a few less decorative flares.

And the taste of its scent on her tongue was like nothing she'd encountered. Rich with promise, buttery and lush. Savory, not sweet. Without a hint of bitterness. That meaty flavor that mushrooms and steaks had. The chef's called it umami. Difficult to explain, but obvious when tasted. And there was a saltiness to it, with a hint of pepper under that. The buttery richness was the most distinct flavor, though.

A scent she would never forget now that she had tasted it.

Yet, she realized, she wasn't craving that flavor like food. It didn't trigger hunger or the desire to devour the egg. At least…not yet. And for that, she was grateful.

That craving was something she'd have to face one day. But she hoped later rather than sooner. Because just then, the scent of that egg was glorious in a way that she could enjoy without it horrifying her.

The man studied her as she studied the egg. "You do not want to devour it."

"I do not." Though he hadn't asked, only commented. "But I am starting to understand why she does."

"Still repulsed by the idea, though."

Again, just a comment. So she didn't respond. She flicked the leather flap back over and let the man latch it closed again so she didn't risk dropping the egg. Then she slipped the rucksack onto her back so she could keep her hands free to hold onto the three during the fight home.

"Once you have the tribute, return to the river where you first met the three," the man said. "Never bring the youngling with you. Just the tribute. You will be returned here to ensure the tribute meets your dam's expectations. Once it has, our business is done. For now."

"For always." But she wasn't convinced of those words. Still, she did mean them for now. For this youngling and for Hamish. For now, they were done.

"How will you raise it?" The man tilted his head to one side, meeting her gaze. Giving her the vague impression of a bird in that moment, his dark black hair fluttering in the cold breeze in a way that made her think of the three's feathers.

"As what they are. My sibling. The way Hamish

raised me." She would teach her sibling to skip rocks on the river, just as Hamish had done for her. And maybe, one day, when the quickening came, they'd both remember enough of themselves not to destroy their eggs. Maybe they could avoid their dam's fate.

Maybe.

But for now, she would be happy to have a cure for Hamish, or at least the thing he needed to delay his own quickening a bit longer. She figured he wouldn't even scold her too much for defying his wishes and offering the tribute. Not if it saved him. Especially since she was returning alive.

And, best of all, they'd have a little brother or sister to raise. Another person to love. Expanding their little family.

Their family of dragons of some kind.

They Call Her Anger

Anger

They called her Anger. It was as good a name as any. Anger was what she felt most of the time. Not always. There was that one time, three centuries ago, when she'd just woken and a small baby mammal was bouncing around outside her cave, rolling in the dirt trying to wrestle a broken branch. That had been sweet and amusing. She'd spent a good amount of time watching that baby mammal play, and feeling content and quiet, no rage in her head.

Then the baby left and the rage returned. She didn't really mind. Rage was normal. Rage fed the fire. But the time watching the furry bundle of energy had also been nice.

Anger didn't come out of her cave much these

days. It was noisy and everything smelled funny. Hotter, too, though she liked that part. The sunshine seemed to have more power and that felt delicious on her scales. She was still angry when soaking up the sun, but it was the closest she got to content in her rage.

The locals all knew she was there, in a cave half buried under the desert sands now. They gave her a wide berth, or occasionally left her something nice to eat. The last time the women had brought her a whole cow. That was considerate of them. She felt no need to destroy them. Most of them were just trying to live their lives. But it was considerate of them to remember the old ways and ensure she didn't have to leave her cave.

Maybe considerate wasn't quite the right word.

They still told stories of the last time she'd left her cave. When there's been a rash of so-called "witch" murders. The "witches" were just women, and even a small handful of men, who knew how to tend to the others in their community with medicines and herbs. They were the wise people. The learned people. Some just the queer people. And killing someone for their knowledge hit directly into the center point of Anger's rage. She liked when humans learned things, gathered knowledge. Anger hoarded knowledge the way she hoarded little bobbles and bits that she found interesting to look at. Her treasures.

She didn't like when humans killed other humans for just wanting knowledge. Not when it happened so close to her home. She *hated* when they screamed "witch" and murdered people they'd given that label.

The murders stopped after that. And she was given an entire herd of goats for tribute. That went a small way to mollifying her. She'd slept then. Releasing so much rage at once always required a good nap after.

When she woke from her nap, there was someone, a woman, outside her cave. The woman was throwing rocks. Big heavy rocks. Not at her cave. Just at the ground. There was screaming. And shouting. And the hard thump of rock against rock. Anger listened for a while, wondering at the woman's rage.

Then she rose and poked her head out of her cave, watching some more. The rage was on full display. The woman's face was red. She was sweating. Her dark hair glistened with it. The sun was low in the sky as dawn approached, but it wasn't quite day yet. And already this woman raged.

Anger could feel the powerful emotion in the human woman, and she was curious. "Why did you wake me?"

The woman dropped the rock she was about to throw and turned to face the cave, her eyes wide. Sweat dripped down her temples. Her hair was plastered to her cheeks and neck. She seemed unaware of the way her clothing was clinging to her skin and covered in the orange desert dirt.

This woman was one of the paler-skinned humans. The people nearest her cave had many colors and shapes and sizes. Anger liked all those colors. Like the many-colored puppies and dogs that sometimes came near her cave. Everything from the palest of sand, almost white, all the way to a brown so dark it was nearly black. Always browns and tans, though. No pleasant blues or greens, like her own scales, or like some of the birds that occasionally landed in the bushes outside her cave. Which was fine. Anger enjoyed the ranges of browns. Some bright orange or red would have been nice. But humans didn't come in those colors.

The rock-throwing woman's skin was a light tan, and her hair was dark brown. She looked delicate compared to other animals, but for a human not frail. Some of the humans looked like a sharp breeze would break them in half. This one didn't. And she'd had the strength to throw around some sizable rocks.

She didn't cower away from Anger either. Didn't run away screaming. She stood with her hands balled into fists at her sides and stared at Anger with wide eyes, her chin up.

"I didn't mean to wake you, ancient one," the woman said. "I was...upset and needed to release some of my emotions so I don't scare my niece and nephew."

"You have no children of your own to scare?"

"I do not."

"A choice or a happenstance?"

"A choice."

Fair enough. Anger had not chosen to reproduce yet either. She was content with only one of her in the world. And the world was probably saver for that.

"Why do you rage?" Anger asked.

"There are...changes happening in our community, and I do not like them."

"What kind of changes?"

"There are people, men... They wish to relegate the women to property. Not fully human. Property! They think we are not worthy of an equal standing in our society, even though it would not even *exist* if not for us! They would know nothing! If not for us." The woman's jaw tightened, her fists trembled.

The feel of her rage wrapped warmly around Anger. Heating the sand under them. "Why should they wish this?"

"Bah!" The woman threw her hand out,

releasing the emotion trembling through her body. "They call us weak. *Us!* They feel superior. They think they are smarter. Stronger. Faster. Better. They feel some god has given them the right to be highest in society. A god they make up. One who was never in our pantheon before."

Anger knew little of gods, especially the gods of humans. She didn't care for the idea of them and had never met one. She was occasionally treated as a god, but she wasn't one. She was a dragon. And to honor her with food and careful awareness seemed infinitely wiser than worshiping something that wouldn't set your village afire if irritated.

"And *then*," the woman went on, in full rant now, "they claim this is for *our* own good. That they will be our protectors and we must obey or be punished. What kind of protector is that? And what do we need a protector from but them! I would have no need of a 'protector' if not for their threats."

The woman started pacing, stalking around the flat, rocky space outside Anger's cave. She kicked rocks and gestured widely with her hands. "They want power over us, and they will use violence to get it, and *that* is not for *my* own good."

The woman whirled and faced Anger. "And the worst part," she said, her voice a low growl, tight and deep and filled with suppressed violence, "is that they will take our knowledge. They wish us ignorant. They want to take our books, stop teaching our girls to read. Insist the knowledge be kept only for the men so that they may interpret it for us. No! No! I will not have it!"

The woman screamed then. Not a sound of pain, or shock. But outrage. A warrior's cry before charging into battle. Anger had flown over battles, heard those cries, savored the fury. This woman's fury gave Anger heat. Warmth. Felt very good.

And Anger agreed. It was wrong to keep knowledge from those who wanted to learn. Wrong to demand the learned forget. Wrong to keep people ignorant and hoard knowledge for only a small group. She didn't like this new thing that was happening. Anymore than she'd liked the murdering of so called "witches" those centuries ago.

Apparently, they had not remembered the stories, or had stopped telling them. They would not be attempting these laws had they remembered what lurked in the cave near their dwellings.

"I will not be made a piece of property with no ability to nurture my intellect," the woman said as the remnants of her scream continued past Anger, bouncing off the back of her cave. "I will not allow half our people to become ignorant and secondary. I will not have my niece and nephew grow up in a world where they are not given an equal chance to be who they want to be. I will not allow this group to ruin our whole society so that they can feel superior. I *will not let this happen.*"

The last was yelled at the sky, the woman's head thrown back, her face catching the rays of the rising sun, her voice an echo across the sand dunes.

Anger shifted inside her cave. An idea, one she'd been content to let sit quiet and unused, rose up. She had never intended on reproducing. But perhaps it was time. Perhaps now was that moment. This woman was the first she'd encountered with enough rage to, perhaps, survive it.

"Did you come here to ask for my aid?" the dragon asked as she moved a little farther out of her home. Sands above the cave mouth shifted and gently slid to the rocks. The smell of early earth, the minerally richness of the soil, the woman's sweat and rage, filled the clearing in front of the cave. Rays of the newly risen sun caught on her green scales, winking in the light. The day would be hot and Anger looked forward to that heat.

"I did not," the woman said, letting out a deep, slow breath. "I came to shout my anger into the air. There is little I can do as a loan woman. There are too many of us being convinced of this madness, even other women! I will fight. But I will lose. And

I came here to let the fury of that knowledge out before it consumed me."

"But what if you let it consume you," Anger said. "What if you let it simmer and boil inside you, fueling your fight? And what if, that simmering fury gave you strength? And…more."

"More?" The woman frowned but stepped closer. No hesitance at all.

Inside, Anger smiled. "You would be changed, but you would have power. The power of fire. Strength. Knowledge. You would not be…fully human anymore."

The woman blinked. "I don't understand."

"Of course not. I haven't explained. Is your anger because you wish to take the power you will be denied for yourself? Do you want power over others, as the men in the community are trying to force onto you? Or do you demand justice?"

"I want no power over my fellow people. I only want justice to prevail. And common sense. And a measure of acceptance. And freedom to exist as we are without…punishments."

"There is a cost to this gift I could give you. You would carry this feeling always. Never really releasing it. It can warm you. But some would be driven mad. More dangerous than the thing you now rage against. You must be careful."

"Careful," the woman repeated, taking another few steps closer. "Or it would consume me."

"Yes. It is possible to rage, righteously, without being consumed. But some cannot. That is why I've never thought to pass this gift on before." Anger tilted her head. "I think you can survive, though. I think you would flourish."

"What is this gift? And can it save the women? My niece? My nephew? The people who will be harmed by this new direction?"

"Perhaps." Anger tilted her head in a gesture she'd seen the human's make. "Perhaps not. If not, I can always come and burn your dwellings to the ground and you can start over."

The woman's eyes widened, and for once, she looked nervous. "No. That's unnecessary. At least… yet." And with that "yet" she admitted that a razing of her society might be an option. "But for now, I just want them to stop trying to drag us this direction. To stop with these backward ideas."

"The gift I will give you, it will simmer inside for always. And you will one day feel the need to take flight. To leave and live in isolation. But before you do, you may pass on this gift. Not as I am. You will not change those you gift the way I will change you. Not before your transformation at least. By then, you will have learned enough to understand the gift's many facets and who may or may not be able to tolerate its power."

"You speak of a gift, but what is it? What kind of gift can you give me?"

"Will you accept my offering? Will you accept the strength to continue, to fight, to persevere, to use that fury you feel now, to embrace it and accept it as your own?"

"Is that what you offer? Because I have plenty of anger already, ancient one."

"But I will give you the power to use it."

The woman considered this, her mouth turned down. A gesture Anger knew to mean she was thinking. And that confirmed for Anger that this was the right woman for this gift. Had she taken the power, hungered for it, she would not have been worthy of it. She would have misused it. But this one took the time to consider, to decide if the burden of the gift was worth the benefit.

That she saw there would be burden as well as benefit spoke in her favor.

"I didn't come here for a gift," the woman said slowly. "Or even to ask for help. But…if this gift can help me fight for a better future, I would accept it."

"You must guard against falling victim to it. Guard not to pass it to those who are not able to handle the consequences and burden."

"I will."

"Then I offer you this. It is a righteous burning rage which will feed your fight. You will have strength, knowledge, and power they do not see coming. Clever and dangerous as a dragon itself. Will you accept all this means?"

"I will." The woman faced Anger fully again, her hands no longer fisted, but her chin still raised and her gaze steady.

The sunlight burst over the dunes then, painting the desert in soft oranges and yellows, sparkling golden light on the sand crystals. Yes, Anger decided. It was time to share. Time to spread some of her around a little. Maybe past time.

She dragged in a deep breath, let the fire build in her belly, let the rage grow into a seed. A seed that would grow in the fertile ground that was the woman's own fury.

Then she released the fire, letting it wash over the woman as the morning sun had washed over her. The woman didn't scream, or shout, or cry out. She spread her hands wide and accepted the gift.

The seed was planted.

When the woman returned to her people, Anger went back to sleep. Content. She had not thought to reproduce before meeting this woman. But it was time. Let them try to control those like her. Let them try to murder more "witches." Such things would no longer require the dragon to burn them out. The woman, and those like her, those she passed the gift on to, would do all the work. Perhaps even creating a better society for them all.

But that was for the humans to sort out.

Now, Anger would sleep again, knowing she had ensured the world remembered her. And then, perhaps, they would bring her another cow.

Dragon
Appreciation Day

At the Herpetology Center

Jane's dragons weren't the kind intended when that author created Dragon Appreciation Day. Dragon Appreciation Day was supposed to be about the mythical murder beasts. Fictional creatures that breathed fire and swallowed their prey whole.

Jane's dragons could swallow their prey in large chunks, digesting everything but a few bones and some hair. But they weren't fictional.

And since the zoo had *actual* dragons, and the director of the herpetology center—the Reptile House as they called it—took advantage of every single opportunity to plug his particular exhibits, trying to bring in more money and more prestige for himself, well... Now, the zoo celebrated Dragon Appreciation Day.

Jane didn't mind. She appreciated her dragons every day. Having a specific day when everyone else did too was nice.

According to the Chinese calendar, Jane was also a dragon. Which spoke to a level of irony that amused her. She wasn't Chinese, though, so maybe it didn't count.

The current crush of kids loitering around the thick glass in front of the Komodo dragon enclosure was the seventh school group through here in the last hour. Teenagers this time. Some disinterested. Some excited. It wasn't every day a kid from the Bronx got to see a full grown Komodo dragon. And Jane's dragons were something to behold.

Especially Morana, currently sitting with her face toward the overhead sun lamps, soaking up the heat.

Inside the encloser, the temperature was kept at a balmy ninety degrees, the humidity a constant, muggy seventy percent. Outside, New York's winter had set in big time. There hadn't been any snow for Christmas, but now that they were halfway through January, the temperatures had dropped severely, snow piled in dirty gray hills along the sidewalks, and the wind cut through coats and pants, creating a wind chill that made it feel like single digit temperatures beyond the warm, humid Reptile House.

This time of year, Jane really loved her job. Well, to be fair, she always loved her job. There was nowhere else she'd rather be. This particular habitat, in this particular section of the zoo, with these particular animals. Even the reptilian smell of the place, part musk and dryness, a little hint of predator poop. The underlying scent of rot no one noticed because the pungent smell of reptile was so strong.

She felt at home when she entered this place.

Especially with the Komodos. Especially with Morana.

She and Morana had an understanding that worked out very well for both of them.

With this last group of kids, Morana was front and center behind the thick glass walls of the enclosure, basking in the sun lamps, her massive body on full side display for the gawking teenagers. At six foot in length, weighing in at a hefty hundred and eighty pounds, Morana was a magnificent Komodo. Her armored skin was a speckled green and gray. Her dark green-brown eyes currently closed as she took in the heat from artificial sun. Occasionally, her gray forked tongue flickered out to taste the air.

Almost dinner time, Jane thought. Just one more tour, my girl. Then we'll get to our main meal. Celebrate the holiday in our own special way.

She had something particularly good for Morana tonight.

But it had to wait until they were alone.

The guide leading the high schoolers on their tour fielded questions, but she wasn't the expert herpetologist. That was Jane. That was the reason Jane stood to the side of the group, an invisible presence, there to answer the tougher questions. The guide—Sandra—was not invisible. She was that sort of gorgeous, perky, blond-haired kind of young woman everyone noticed. Even in her standard zoo worker khakis. The tan pants and t-shirt that blended Jane into the background made Sandra look like she belonged on a movie set. A movie about zoo keepers. That could be fun. Probably done before, though.

The director of the herpetology center, when he came into the room, was not the sort of person easily overlooked either. At over six foot tall, physically fit, dressed in dark slacks and a light blue, short-sleeve t-shirt, his blond-brown hair perfectly combed, his sharp blue eyes open and attentive to the teenagers, he commanded attention. Lots and lots of attention. From everyone. Including Sandra.

"How's everyone doing today?" he said in his booming voice, clapping his hands together.

Jane winced, the sound much too loud for her ears, but no one noticed.

"This place is amazing," one girl said, batting her eyes at the director.

He preened under the teenager's attention and at her compliment. "We work very hard to ensure the health and well-being of our animals, don't we, Sandra?"

"Absolutely, director," Sandra said in her chipper tour guide voice.

Though her expression as she glanced at the director was less chipper zoo employee, more… Well, Jane thought of that expression as the filled-with-innuendo expression. The director was married, but that didn't seem to matter to Sandra. Or the director for that matter.

Having him here in person was unusual on a normal day. He didn't lower himself to the day-to-day maintenance and care for the animals. That was Jane's job. Especially with the Komodos. Especially with Morana.

But this wasn't a normal day. Dragon Appreciation Day was top of his holiday list for raising money for the center. And it all started with ensuring the school kids were happy and enthusiastic about *real* dragons. So they'd go home and tell their parents all about the dragons. This wasn't just any ordinary school outreach tour. These were the kids from the private schools, and the hard-to-get-into public schools. The places where rich parents could be found, parents with deep pockets to support a kid's favorite new species. These were the schools the city saw as important, and so provided endowments and grants and funding for events like this. This outreach was specifically calculated to raise money.

So long as her dragons saw the benefit of all that manipulation and schmoozing, Jane was happy to celebrate the holiday. She kept her feelings about the director, and her feelings about the cacophony of teenagers, to herself and smiled—even though no one looked at her—and answered questions when Sandra couldn't.

And made sure everyone moved through the area in a timely manner.

Jane and Morana had made this particular holiday special, an event the two of them had celebrated in their special way for the last...five years now. But that only happened after the tours were gone and there was no one left around to notice.

Jane was the only one Morana tolerated. The other keepers couldn't get near her without Morana hissing and chasing them away. A nearly two hundred pound hissing reptile who could put on a sudden burst of speed, had skin like chainmail, and serrated teeth that could crunch through skin and bone like butter was the kind of animal keepers moved carefully around. Avoided going into the habitat with them if they could.

But Morana and Jane had an understanding. If Jane were the fanciful sort, she might call them soulmates. Probably not any more appropriate than thinking herself a dragon because of the year she was born under the Chinese calendar. Still. They were two of a kind. Dragons no one could get close to. Dragons who stuck together.

Unlike Jane, though, Morana didn't blend into the background unless she wanted to. Her excellent gray-green skin color and pattern let her hide if she chose to rest near the back of the enclosure in the tall grass. When she wanted to be on display, Morana put herself on display. And she was magnificent.

Jane never reached that level of display, herself. She wasn't someone people noticed. Even without trying, she blended into her surroundings. Was mostly invisible. That was fine. She didn't need to be noticed. Didn't *want* to be notice most of the time.

"I've heard they eat people," one teenager said into the din of chatter. "Do they really eat people?"

Sandra gave Jane a wide-eyed look, that stiff

expression she got when she didn't have a good answer to a question.

"They're predators," Jane said, drawing everyone's attention for the first time during this tour. "They're always dangerous. And they've been known to attack and kill humans before. But they're more likely to eat carrion than go after a full grown human adult."

"What's carrion?" the boy asked, his dark eyes gleaming.

"Carrion is dead meat. Sometimes rotten. The kind of thing vultures eat, for example. Komodo dragons are opportunistic. They'll eat whatever comes to hand." The teenager looked a little disappointed, which made the director frown, so Jane added, "They have been known to dig up graves and eat the corpses."

That got a lot of attention. Some squealing and ewwing from the girls. A few too-enthusiastic "gross!"es from the boys. The kid who'd asked about Komodos eating people stared at her avidly.

"Really?" he said.

"If the grave is shallow, they'll dig up the body and eat it. A problem for the people living on the islands where the Komodo is native. And since it's a protected species, they can't do anything about it. They've had to change where they bury their dead, to soil that's harder for the dragons to dig in, and sometimes they pile rocks on top of the graves to keep the dragons out. But if a Komodo can get at an easy meal of dead meat, it will happily devour that meal."

The kid's eyes widened more and more as she spoke. When she finished, he looked very excited. "Cool," he breathed.

He returned his avid gaze to Morana. He even reached out and touched the glass separating him from the giant reptile. Morana flickered her tongue out, tasting the air again, and red saliva dripped from her mouth. The girl standing next to the avid boy so interested in corpse eating made a squeaky noise and turned away from Morana.

But the boy leaned closer to the glass and said, "Its spit looks like blood." There was awe in his voice.

That much excitement over corpse eating and red saliva. He'd either grow up to be a herpetologist or a serial killer. Either way, he was probably going to need some therapy.

Which reminded Jane, she needed to call her therapist.

After the holiday. Today was a special day.

"Scientists used to think the bacteria in their mouths caused their prey to get sick and die," Jane said, "even if it escaped the Komodo's initial attack. But recent research suggests they're venomous. They have venom glans, and the venom has an anti-coagulant element to it."

"What's that mean?" the boy asked, still staring at Morana. The Komodo's head was lifted so it was on level with the boy's chest.

"The venom prevents blood clotting," Jane said. "The prey bleeds to death even if it gets away from the dragon."

The boy turned to look at her and Jane quickly refocused on his face.

"What kind of prey?" he asked.

"Mostly things like goats, pigs, deer, other Komodo dragons."

"They eat each other?" The kid was leaning closer to her now, hanging on her every word.

It was the most attention she'd had from any of these kids all day. The longest anyone had bothered to even look her in a while. Although, she suspected the kid wasn't actually seeing her. She suspected there were other thoughts filling his imagination. The ones that were going to require therapy.

"Sometimes," she said. "They eat the young ones. That's why Komodo babies live in trees for the first four or five years of their lives. Trying to escape hungry adults."

"Wow." The boy looked at Morana again. "It eats deer here?"

"At the zoo, she's fed mostly mice and rabbits and rats."

"Ew," the girl standing next to the avid boy said. "You feed it rabbits? But rabbits are so cute."

"Good food," the boy said. Which made the girl squeal again. He smiled without looking at her.

"I heard they get rotten meat stuck in their mouth," he said, looking at Jane again.

"No. They're actually very conscientious about cleaning their mouth and face after they eat. No blood or rotten flesh left behind." Jane loved that about her dragons. They were very neat and tidy. So very thorough.

Another kid from farther down the glass pointed to something inside the enclosure. "What's that?"

Sandra turned to look, smiled, and said, "Ah, Jane, why don't you take this one?"

Sandra really didn't know much of anything about the Komodos. But then her knowledge wasn't the reason she had this job.

Jane moved farther into the throng of teenagers. The boy pointed at a tangled lump of material, a mixture of hair, grass, and other things. "That's a gastric pellet," she said. "Komodos digest almost all of what they eat, and they swallow entire animals, but they can't completely digest hair and horns and bones. So they spit them back up."

More ews and grosses erupted behind and around her. One kid took the coat he'd been carrying over his arm and covered his head with it.

"Is that why it looks like there's a finger bone in that thing?" the avid boy who'd been so fascinated with corpse eating said.

Jane took a closer look at the chunk of hair and grass and other things, frowning.

"I'm sure it's just a left over rabbit bone," the director said with his big, bright smile. "Why don't we move on to the next exhibit. Plenty to see. We have an eight foot long boa constrictor right next door. And then we'll get to the bearded dragons."

That got a lot of excited chatter from the kids—they probably didn't know bearded dragons were tiny compared to a Komodo. The group turned toward the door leading to the rest of the reptile center, talking over each other as they pushed and shoved and laughed their way out of the Komodo exhibit's viewing area.

The avid boy hesitated as he stared first at the pellet, then at Morana. "Real life dragons are so much better than myths," he murmured.

Jane agreed with that.

The director, standing a few feet from Jane, hunted the room before spotting her, blinking as if she'd appeared out of nowhere instead of having been standing right there the whole time.

"Ah. Yes. Uh." He glanced at the name tag on her uniform shirt. "Jane. There you are. Don't forget to feed our girl. Time for a nice big meal, isn't it?"

He didn't wait for her answer, instead, putting a hand on Sandra's lower back and guiding her from the room as they followed the school group.

Jane watched them go. Silent. Until even the reluctant avid boy had disappeared.

"I have a special holiday meal for Morana, director," she said to the now empty room outside the enclosure. "Don't worry. I always make sure she gets something good on this day."

Jane faced Morana. The Komodo's tongue flickered as she tasted the air. Then she turned to face Jane through the glass.

Jane flickered her tongue out too. Tasting the residual flavors of everyone scents on the air. The pheromones the director and Sandra had been giving off.

One of these days, the director's wife was going to kill him for all his philandering. Murder him in his sleep. Maybe poison him. Jane wouldn't blame the woman. The director's wife was a lot like her. Easy to overlook. Easy to ignore. Easy to miss in a crowd. The kind of person who could get away with murdering her husband if she were very careful. She could even make it look like a disappearance instead of a murder. Couldn't be a murder without a body, right?

And if…when the woman did murder her husband, Jane might suggest a very efficient way to dispose of the body. So long as the director's wife didn't use poison, that is. Jane had spent five years getting the process just right, ensuring nothing but the occasional finger bone remained. Those were easy to clean up and throw out without anyone being the wiser. Only the occasional eagle-eyed kid ever spotted those kinds of things anyway.

Certainly no one expected these dragons to actually eat anything that had fingers. Or that the quiet, invisible dragon keeper might feed her dragons anything but the prescribed zoo diet.

And what use all her years of practice if she didn't share her knowledge with other invisible women, right? Other dragons in hiding, needing to dispose of their enemies.

"We know how to celebrate Dragon Appreciation Day," she murmured. "Don't we? We dragons stick together."

Morana's tongue flicked the air again.

Jane smiled. "Special meal coming right up. You'll like this one. He was a real asshole. To his wife. To his kids. Nasty piece of work. But tasty. You'll enjoy your share." She headed toward the side door that took her into the backrooms, to the food prep area with the large, industrial freezer. To prepare the special meal that she and Morana would share.

But she paused to touch the glass near Morana's face.

"Happy Dragon Appreciation Day, my girl."

Imagining Things

CHAPTER ONE

Standing in the middle of his kitchen, staring at the door that led into the basement, every single horror movie and book that Jaylen had ever read ran through his head. He went down into the basement, he might as well be wearing skimpy clothes and high heels, a Too Stupid To Live heroine at her finest, just gleefully tripping down the steps to "investigate a strange sound," on her way to her death by the deranged serial killer waiting in the basement.

Or, or! He was the cop standing at the top of the stairs, about to discover the missing person stashed away in the basement, only to have the serial killer stab him in the back—literally—and kill him. Probably that one was more appropriate to his situation. Except he wasn't a cop. And as far as he knew, there were no missing persons stashed in his own basement.

So yeah, maybe the first was the real problem.

A loud thump sounded below him. Loud enough to make him jump. That wasn't a mouse or even a rat. Too loud for that. Something much bigger was thumping around down there. And it wasn't his furnace. Which was busted and he had to get fixed still. Logical explanations, like boxes falling over, or the washing machine throwing a fit, were non-starters since he had neither boxes nor a washing machine in his basement. His basement was basically a large, open, cement floor that stretched the length of his relatively modest two bedroom ranch and was home to his currently not working furnace and one, repeat one, old suitcase with a broken handle that he'd been meaning to throw out since his last business trip and kept forgetting about.

None of which should be making that loud thumping noise he'd been hearing for the last half hour and trying to ignore so he didn't live out the Too Stupid To Live heroine trope.

He was not a brave man. He was the kind of man who stood back and let other people investigate strange noises. People who were brave and had less imagination.

Imagination was the problem, see. Jaylen's was what one might call…strong. Impressive even. And, well, dangerous. No one would argue with that description if they actually knew about Jaylen's imagination and what it could *really* do.

For the most part, he used that imagination to draw panels for graphic novels and comic books, channeling his considerable imagination into something that made him money but which he could shut off without getting into trouble. That paid for his moderately comfortable life, required he travel to conferences to be around other people only occasionally, and ensured he had someplace to put his imagination without danger. Normally, that was enough.

Right now, his imagination was threatening to get away from him. And that was bad.

Another loud thump from the basement sent his pulse racing and sweat dripped down his cheeks. His cellphone was plugged in in the living room. He was in the kitchen. It would take him about twenty seconds to sprint back to his phone and call the police. He could do that. Just go call the police and say there was a strange noise in his basement. They might not shoot him on sight when they arrived. They might listen to him, believe he owned this home, actual investigate the noise in his basement. Discover it was something they needed to handle.

For all he knew, it was a huge animal that had somehow gotten down there and got trapped. That would require animal control, right? Or an escaped convict. Definitely a job for the police. Or maybe a serial killer setting up a torture room…

No. Okay. He had to stop or something horrible really would happen.

Reining in his imagination took effort. A few deep breaths, filled with the lingering scent of the delicious pork tacos he'd made for dinner—if that was the last thing he smelled, it wouldn't be a bad thing. He could go out on pork tacos being his last meal. He'd rather *not* of course. But that part wouldn't be a lingering regret. He would regret passing on the pralines and cream ice cream in his fridge since he was trying to lose some of the weight he put on over the last two years. Doctor's orders. But if he died tonight, he was gonna be pissed he didn't eat the ice cream.

Another deep breath. Okay. So. Call the cops—and risk them shooting him before he could explain the problem. Keep standing here like an idiot—and wait for the danger to come up the stairs and kill him. Investigate the strange noise—and possibly be killed by a serial killer.

Yeah, no, none of this was good.

Still, the more he stood here, the more likely his imagination was to get away from him, so he had to just…do something. Anything.

He looked toward the living room, visible

through the open entry into the kitchen. The television was still on, but muted—he'd muted it when he'd heard the noise the first time—and he could see the baseball game still on but he couldn't see the score from here. Which was fine. His team was losing. He'd rather not know how badly if he was about to die.

Stop it! He wanted to smack himself across the face. He was talking nonsense. It was probably just some animal who'd found a way in and gotten stuck. Maybe brought a branch into the basement and was thunking it around, looking for a way out. Something innocuous like that. Nothing he needed to be panicking about.

Okay. This was it. He was going to man up, so to speak, and head down there.

He glanced around the kitchen. Then went to the cabinet next to the sink where he kept a flashlight. It was one of those huge steel ones that took a bunch of C batteries, the kind that looked like an old-fashioned truncheon. He hefted it in his hands. The batteries were fresh—he checked them regularly because he did occasionally lose power during winter storms—but he was more interested in the weight of the thing. It would make a decent weapon. And was better than going downstairs without any weapon at all, like the proverbial Too Stupid To Live heroine he absolutely was not.

He jumped as another loud thump sounded from the basement. If that was a ghost, he was moving. He was moving across the country. Tonight. House and possessions be damned.

Would a ghost be better than a serial killer, though? Maybe. He could probably run away from a ghost a lot faster than he might be able to get away from a serial killer. Couldn't hit a ghost with a giant flashlight, so that was a drawback. But also, there was nothing really in the basement for a ghost to knock over on him or hit him with. Except the old suitcase. And the broken furnace. So he just had to stay away from the broken furnace was all.

He straightened his shoulders, ignored the loud sound of his own pulse in his ears, and approached the basement door with his flashlight raised.

Chapter Two

When Jaylen threw open the basement door, he flung himself back against the wall, heart pounding so hard he worried about a heart attack. Wouldn't that be an epic irony. Giving himself a heart attack over a noise that may or may not be life threatening.

The thumping noise went silent. A cold shiver traveled across Jaylen's shoulders, turning his sweat to icy frost.

Shit shit shit. Okay.

He took a couple of deep, panting breaths and then swung into the open doorway and flicked on the basement light all in one move. Bright lights lit up the previously pitch black basement. No swinging lights or bad bulbs for his basement. He'd changed the bulbs in the series of overhead track lighting that kept the basement from being a shadow-filled nightmare. Despite its size, and being a generally neglected part of his home, it was *not* a place filled with dark corners in which a serial killer could hide.

This was not his first rodeo.

From his vantage at the top of the stairs, all he could see was the empty cement floor that stretched out from the base of the last step. The broken furnace would be to the left. Nothing but open space to the right. The stairs were wooden but closed, so they didn't have that gap in between them that would give someone hiding under the stairs an opening to, say, grab a hapless hero by the ankle and send him tumbling to his death at the base of the stairs.

Taking his first step onto the top step, however, took an act of will. He trembled as he took the second step, holding the flashlight in front of him like a staff. "Anyone down there?" he asked, then winced.

What was a serial killer going to say? "Yes, I'm here. I'm expecting you."

Fuck that would be creepy. Maybe that is what a serial killer would say. Or a ghost might say something equally creepy. Like, "I've been waiting for you Jaylen…"

His breathing came in pants as he once again

reigned in his imagination before he actually started to hear those spooky sentences. No. Wasn't going to go there. He had been working with his imagination for his whole life. He could do this without making it worse. Remember, probably just an animal that came in through one of the low windows and got trapped. It froze when the door had banged open suddenly because it was scared and that's what animals do.

A trapped animal would be more scared of him than he was of it, he tried to remind himself as he hurried down the next few stairs. The tension and waiting and not knowing was getting to him. He had to get this over with. Had to know what was down here. When he found out, *then* he could do the next thing.

And if that next then was run away screaming, so be it. He could do that. Toss his flashlight at the serial killer and run like the track star his high school gym teacher had wanted him to be even though he hated running.

He reached the bottom stair and looked around the open basement fast, hurried, hunting out the source of the noise as quickly as possible. Waving the flashlight in front of himself to hit anything that rushed him before he could see it.

Nothing. Nothing that he could see anyway.

But... There had to be something that had been

making that noise. He stayed on the bottom step, leery of stepping too far into the basement and getting trapped. But he hunted the narrow windows near the basement ceiling. Four all together. Two across from the stairs and two to the right, opposite the furnace. No tree branches or random bushes bumping them in the wind—he knew that wouldn't be the noise. He kept all the bushes and trees away from the windows and it wasn't a windy night anyway.

He searched the area around the broken furnace, the only place where someone might hide. From his place on the stairs, he couldn't see behind it, and the tall collection of metal boxes and copper and insulated pipes wasn't exactly small. There could have been a fully grown adult hiding behind it, he supposed.

They'd have to be pretty skinny, though. That, at least, would give Jaylen the weight advantage. He couldn't have hidden behind the furnace without being noticed. His head might have stuck out over the top a little. And even turned sideways and pressed up against the wall, he wasn't sure he'd have been able to keep himself hidden.

Still, he searched the shadows in and around the furnace. Nothing he could see. No weird waving shadows, like someone standing there trying not to move.

If it was an animal, though, that was the place to hide. He might not spot a trapped animal hiding there. Not from the stairs. So he was going to have to go hunt the area around the furnace. And he did not want to do that.

Stalling, he searched the open cement floor again. Solid gray, smooth, but uncomfortable. One day, he might finish down here and turn it into a gaming room or something. A man cave. Except his whole house was his man cave and he really didn't like basements. He thought he'd be okay having one when he bought this house. He had misjudged his tolerance for them.

There wasn't anything slithering or ducking into corners of the open room. The only other thing down here was the broken suitcase that he'd tossed against the...

Oh. It wasn't where he thought he'd left it.

That wasn't good.

He was almost positive he'd tossed that suitcase against the wall next to the furnace after his last trip, when the extension handle had broken hours before his flight home, leaving him no time to get another bag. The soft-sided, large black bag had managed to fit all the things he needed—clothes, comics, sample art, postcards he gave away. There was some silver duct tape on one corner, where the material had ripped on his second to last trip, and the four wheels were a little weird now, so when he dragged it on all four at once it moved sideways instead of straight. But it had functioned okay and was useable until the extension handle broke.

Once that happened, he'd had to just roll it using the short handle on top and that had been awkward because at his height, he'd had to lean over to grab it. Not fun once he'd collected the bag from the airport. After emptying it when he got home, he'd carried it down here and left it by the furnace promising himself he'd throw it out the next time he took the trash out. He didn't want it cluttering his space upstairs. And he wanted to search the pockets one more time before throwing it out, in case he left something inside he didn't want to lose.

The bag was about two feet away from the wall now. Not leaning against the wall where he'd left it.

It was possible he'd moved the bag at some point in the last few weeks. Come down to look at the furnace brand thinking he'd get it fixed soon. Just…came down to make sure the basement was still empty. Except he hadn't been in the basement since throwing the bag down here. He knew he hadn't. Or he would have remembered to throw it out at least once in the last few weeks. But it was still here. Because he hadn't been in the basement.

So the bag shouldn't have moved. Who would have moved it?

Terror shot through his entire body and the urge to run upstairs, slam the door, lock it, and push the fridge in front of it was strong. So strong he actually froze and couldn't run away. Typical horror movie reaction for the dumb schmuck about to get killed.

The flashlight in his hand shook. He firmed his grip on it and tried not to hyperventilate, but he was breathing so fast he was starting to see spots. Damn it, he was freaking himself out. With no obvious signs of anything wrong except a moved suitcase. This was ridiculous. He was a grown man. And he was letting his imagination get the best of him. Again. Which was dangerous. He was not supposed to do that.

Okay. Okay. So. He could just…go look at the bag. Again, it was probably just some animal who had gotten in through one of the windows. It didn't matter that they weren't obviously broken and he kept them locked. Animals did weird things. Strange things happened. Maybe there was a whole somewhere he couldn't see. It was probably just a… a raccoon maybe. That would suck. Raccoons could have rabies. He didn't want a raccoon in his house.

But at least it would be a realistic and ordinary situation. He could go back upstairs, close the basement door, and call animal control. They wouldn't shoot him. And he'd get the raccoon out without issue.

He took a few quick breaths, gearing himself up to approach the suitcase. This was fine. Everything was fine.

Swallowing, he took that last step off the stairs and approached the bag. The top looked unzipped. He'd left it open, hadn't he? Hadn't zipped it back up. He thought he might have actually zipped it closed, but he didn't remember, so he could have left it open.

The closer he got, the more his flashlight hand shook. He cursed in his head, afraid to say anything aloud, and reached toward the bag with his flashlight. Another rapid series of breaths, like he was about to plunge into freezing water, and he flipped the top flap of the suitcase open.

The sound of his screech echoed on the basement walls as something leapt out of the bag. Right at him.

CHAPTER THREE

J aylen scrambled backward, swinging the large flashlight at the thing that had jumped out of his suitcase, desperately trying to put space between the thing and himself. He couldn't even have said what the thing was. It could have been a raccoon. It could have been a bat. It could have been a serial killer of diminutive size. He was too panicked in those first few minutes to even know.

He reached the stairs but was too terrified to turn and run up them. The thing, whatever the hell it was, might get him from behind if he turned his back on it. Several moments of swinging his flashlight from the bottom stairs step, his free hand gripping the wooden banister, passed before he got a decent view of his assailant.

Not a raccoon. Not a bat.

He still wasn't sure what it was. Small, yes. But with lots of teeth in a large mouth. Head about twice the size of its body. A grayish skin color under rough brown hair, or fur. A long tail with a spike on the end. And claw tipped limbs—six of them. It sort of ran on its back four legs while reaching for Jaylen with its front legs like arms. The claws tipping its fingertips were black and winked sharply in the basement's track lighting. The stench of sewage followed the thing, whatever it was, a smell so bad Jaylen thought his dinner might come back up again.

The creature screeched at him and leapt backward, so it was standing near the suitcase but more in the middle of the open basement. "Give it back!"

Jaylen froze in mid flashlight-swing. It had talked. He hadn't been hearing things, right? That… whatever that was had just spoken.

"Give it back!"

Yup. Definitely spoken.

"Give…w-what back?" His voice sounded thick and too high, but he was too scared to even clear his throat.

"You stole it."

"I didn't steal anything."

"You did! I saw it. In your books. I saw it. You have it. You stole it."

"What the hell are you talking about?" And what are you? And how are you talking? And how on this good green earth can you be real?! But the last he didn't say out loud. He was too terrified of the answers.

"You stole the egg. You stole it. And it's mine! I earned it. I want it back."

"Egg?" He hunted the basement, trying to figure out what the little creature was talking about. "I have some eggs upstairs. Is that all you want?"

"The *dragon* egg," the creature said, snarling. "Don't want your stupid chicken eggs. What good are those to me. I want the *dragon* egg."

Dragon egg? Oh no. This was definitely not really happening. Maybe he'd given himself a stroke and he was in the hospital now, dreaming all this as he fought death on a ventilator. That would make more sense than the smelly gray creature looking for a dragon egg.

"I saw it in your book. You think I didn't? I know you have it. You couldn't have drawn that and not have it. It's mine. I have waited centuries for that egg. You have it. I know you do."

One of the recent comics he'd been drawing for was an epic fantasy adventure series. There were dragons involved. He might have drawn a dragon egg in one of the last editions. "I…" He shook his head. "What I draw isn't real. It's just fiction."

That's how his imagination *stayed* fiction. He got it out into a form that was supposed to be fiction. His brain *knew* those creations were fiction. And that ensured his imagination had a safe outlet. Without that outlet, things could go very wrong very fast. But the things he drew were absolutely *not* real. That was the entire point.

"Then how did you get the color right? Hmm? How did you get the size and shape and design right? Hmm? You have it. And it's mine."

"First, I was just drawing an egg. Second, I didn't do the final colorizing. That was another artist. Third, eggs all kind of look similar, right?"

"Not dragon eggs! They are specific. They are specific!" The little gray creature launched at Jaylen again.

Jaylen swung out with his flashlight in a panic and it connected with the vicious little being. Not before it got a swing in, though, and scrapped deep enough across Jaylen's hand to draw blood.

Fuck. He hated blood. Seeing real blood made him pass out. He couldn't afford to pass out now. He forced himself not to look at the wound. Later. He could clean it later. First, he had to get rid of this… whatever it was.

But how? This wasn't something animal control

could help him with. And it wasn't something the police would even believe. He'd definitely get shot if he called them for this.

Jesus, would anyone else even see this thing? Was he imagining it? Had he…inadvertently created this situation?

But no. He'd been worried about human serial killers and raccoons. This wasn't even a cross between those two things. This wasn't him. This was…whatever that thing was, but it wasn't something he'd invented. He'd never even imagined something like this.

"Give it back!"

"I don't have anything!" He was panting. And the cut on his hand ached. And he was sweating so hard, the sweat was stinging his eyes. And he had no idea what to do. The creature moved too fast for him to try and race up the stairs to get away from it. And even if he did lock it in the basement, how the hell had it gotten in in the first place? What if it got into the rest of the house?

Panic was shutting down his logical brain, making it difficult to think clearly. And that was also bad because then his imagination might just take over.

"Listen," he said, trying to keep his tone steady. He still sounded too squeaky, but at least he wasn't shouting. "Listen, I have no idea what you want or what you're looking for. I drew a picture, from my imagination, that I made up. I didn't know there was such a thing as real dragon eggs. I certainly don't have one. Wouldn't have stolen one. And there isn't one in my house. You have the wrong guy."

"No one can draw an egg just like a real one out of their imagination," the creature said, his voice a low hissing sort of sound. "They are specific. Each one unique. Each one identifiable. There are only thirteen in the entire world. You could not have drawn one of them without seeing it! Where. Is. It?"

"I. Don't. Have. It." He matched the creatures tenor. "I swear to you. I have no idea what you're talking about. I am too terrified now to lie about this."

The god's honest truth. He couldn't have thought up a lie in that moment if he'd tried.

"You brought it back with you," the creature said. "I saw it in this big ugly bag. I *saw* it."

Jaylen scrambled through his memory, searching for something that could have looked like the drawing of an egg he did in the dragon comic. There wasn't anything. None of the props or pictures he'd taken home had had anything to do with that particular comic. It had been one of his featured books, but most of his focus had been on promoting an upcoming edition of two graphic novels he'd been involved in. One was a fantasy, so that referenced the fantasy comic a bit. He'd signed some of that particular comic series. Had he signed one with the dragon egg? He couldn't remember. It had been several months.

"I have no idea what you're talking about," he said. Again. "I can't even think of anything I brought home that could have looked like that egg. And I swear to you, I swear, I just made that up. I didn't even do the colors on it. Getting the exact egg was pure fluke."

Later, when he wasn't trembling and facing a being out of a nightmare and wasn't worried about that being tearing open his intestines looking for something Jaylen didn't have, he'd think about the fact that there were supposed to be exactly thirteen dragon eggs in the world, and that they all looked very specific, and that one day, since those were eggs, they might hatch. And produce dragons. Dragons.

He sort of hoped he was long dead by the time they did hatch.

"It's mine," the creature said, his voice raspy and deep, his top lip curling. "Mine. Mine to look after. Mine to hatch when the time is right. Mine to make sure it doesn't hatch until the time is right. Mine to guide and ensure its triumph."

"Triumph?" Up to that point, the creature ensuring the egg didn't hatch too soon sounded like a good plan. But "triumph" didn't sound good for the world.

"Mine will be the greatest of the dragons. Will take over all the other twelve and there will dawn a new age of dragons with me as the king."

"I…" That little thing was going to be king with *dragons* behind him? Jaylen only knew imaginary dragons, had no idea what a real dragon might look like, but the general consensus in fiction was that they were large. And this being, claws and deadly teeth and all, was pretty small to control a bunch of dragons.

But what did Jaylen know. He just drew things and tried not to let his imagination loose. Maybe this…whatever he was had the knack for controlling dragons.

"Okay," he said, still trying to placate the creature. "Listen. I don't have a dragon egg. I would have noticed by now. It's been months since I last used that case. I honestly don't have it. If it was ever in there…maybe the people at the airport took it?"

"No. I checked. You think I wouldn't check."

Jaylen's hand was really stinging now and he just wanted to get upstairs and pour rubbing alcohol over the wound. And then maybe go to the hospital for more disinfecting and some stitches. He could feel the blood dripping down his hand, but he didn't want to look away from the creature to check on the injury. The thought of his own blood made him woozy enough anyway. He wasn't sure he *could* look at his hand without passing out. Then he'd bleed out. And no one would know what happened to him.

No. No. Not going to think about that either. Nope.

He tried again. "I don't know how to help you. I don't have a dragon egg."

"I will ring the truth out of you," the creature said, stepping forward.

Jaylen raised his flashlight to defend himself, but he was starting to go fuzzy around the edges, which he blamed on blood loss. This was serious and he needed to do something about this. He had to stop bleeding all over his basement stairs. Especially if he wanted to be able to fend off this…whatever it was that was creeping forward, snarling, showing all those teeth.

Blinking hard, he realized he could imagine a bandage on his hand. Or even imagine it healed. This qualified as an emergency. If he passed out, he wouldn't likely wake up. He needed to do something.

Okay. Okay. He could do this. He let his vision blur. He really didn't want to take his attention from the approaching creature, even though the creature was stalking forward slowly, his attention on

Jaylen's flashlight. So Jaylen kept his gaze forward, toward the creature, a sort of act, pretending to still be watching him. But most of his focus moved inward.

Into his imagination. And that deep well of power.

Chapter Four

Jaylen imagined his wound sealing up, the edges of the slice knitting together as the blood stopped, as the muscle underneath and tendons and veins and arteries closed and combined and fixed. His awareness of anatomy only went so far, but he allowed his imagination to visualize what he needed, what the end result would be. The rest would take care of itself. He pictured the would closing, could feel it closing. Blood stopped dripping down his hand. The painful ache subsided.

He *imagined* his hand feeling normal. Exactly as it always did. Just like the other hand. Exactly as it had been before coming into the basement. Right back to that place when he'd still been in his kitchen.

He poured the weight of his considerable imagination into the *feel* of his hand being healed and normal.

When he was sure it was done, he blinked hard and shook his head, pulling himself out of the trance. The creature had stopped moving closer and was staring at him with narrowed eyes. Jaylen blinked a few more times then glanced down at his hand. Looked perfectly normal now. No cuts. No scars. No blood. There was a little smear of red across his knuckles, bright against his dark skin, and enough to make his stomach roll. But that was it. No other blood on his hand.

He didn't look down at the puddle on the stairs because he didn't want to know how much blood he'd lost. And even though he wasn't still bleeding, blood on the floor would still make him pass out.

He watched the little creature staring at him and wondered if he'd just made a mistake. He wasn't about to bleed to death and felt like he could defend himself again, so that had to be good. But also, he didn't like the way the creature was staring at him now.

"You have magic," the creature said quietly. "You have *the* magic."

"I don't know what you mean." He actually didn't. Which was helpful. He didn't want to admit to anything. But also, he was still unable to think clearly enough to lie.

"*The* magic," the creature said. "Creator magic."

"I'm…an artist. Is that what you mean?" Now he was dancing around the topic. He hadn't heard of creator magic and he didn't know what it was, but he did know what the creature was talking about, so pretending he didn't know was harder.

"Are you still poisoned?"

Jaylen blinked. Poison? There'd been poison in that wound? Shit shit shit. He hadn't thought about that. It hadn't been part of his imagined healing. But…he didn't feel anything anymore. Not even dizzy. So maybe his imagination had healed that too without him having to be specific?

Except usually, his imagination did need some specifics to work right. There had to be detailed feelings and senses and knowledge and images all combined into *reality*. To *make* reality.

He'd made the reality of his wound healing. Of being uninjured and everything normal. The reality of back to the way he'd been before. So hopefully that got rid of the poison, too.

"I don't think so," he said, honestly. He wasn't certain but he kind of thought he might not have any poison in him anymore because of the way he'd imagined his hand healing.

"Hmmm." The creature's eyes narrowed so

much, they nearly disappeared into his gray face. The rough brown hair around his head and jaw bunched together. And silence held for a long moment. Then, "You made the egg! There's a new one. You made a new one. A twin. That's it. It's not mine. It's the fourteenth! We didn't know how that one would come to be. The others were laid down at the dawn of time on this planet but only the thirteen and there were supposed to be fourteen. We thought we'd lost it. Couldn't find it. It had been destroyed. But you made it. You made it!"

Jaylen held both hands up now, no longer using his once-wounded hand to hold the banister and keep him upright. "I didn't create anything. I drew some pictures. But I didn't *make* an egg. I don't have one."

"You *did*," the creature said. "You don't know it. But you did…" His brown eyes narrowed even more and a smile lifted his mouth that showed off all those teeth. "And if you can make one, you can make more."

"I didn't make any."

But the creature wasn't listening now. "You can make all the eggs. Why only thirteen when we can have twenty, thirty. So many dragons."

The last sounded like a really bad idea to Jaylen, but the creature seemed mesmerized and delighted by the idea.

"We've waited millions of years. Guarded the eggs. They will hatch one day and the age of dragons will be upon is. Only fourteen were created, you see. And we lost one. But thirteen. They thought thirteen would be enough. But with you… we can have them all. You just have to create them."

"No." Jaylen didn't want an age of dragons. The age of Man was bad enough. Or age of Human. Whatever. His species were bad enough. Dragons would be horrible. He couldn't imagine that being a peaceful time. Except maybe for the dragons after they'd burnt the rest of the planet to the ground. Well, whenever the dragons hatched, he didn't want to be responsible for there being more than the original fourteen. And he definitely hadn't created one already. He was sure of that.

"You don't have a choice," the creature said, stalking closer again.

Jaylen raised his flashlight. Without the injury on his hand, he could grip the banister tighter, and he was shaking a little less. That was good. He still wasn't sure how to get out of this, but he wouldn't be forced to create dragon eggs.

"You can't beat them out of me," he said. "So I can't be coerced."

"Bribed, then," the creature said, with a wider, and frankly more terrifying smile. "What do you want, small man?"

"Small man?" That was one thing people didn't call Jaylen. Small. He wasn't like, his brother the linebacker huge, but he wasn't exactly a fly away in the wind small either. Well fed and substantial as his grandmother would say. And while not as tall as his brother, he wasn't short. There was more than enough of him to qualify as larger than "small man." Especially when the terrifying creature was actually pretty small itself.

"Would you like gold? I can get you gold? Precious jewels. Or just some of your ordinary paper currency? Easy. You could be rich. Influential. A king."

"No," he said again.

All of that sounded horrible. Well not the extra money. Money was very useful and he didn't mind having it. But influential and a king? No. Also, too much money and people started bothering you about it. He had a hard enough time at conferences sometimes convincing fans he wasn't rich just because he'd drawn some of their favorite comics. Really, being rich felt like it would come with more trouble than he wanted in his life. Enough money to pay his bills and let him travel comfortably when he did have to go places and allow him to keep doing a job that he was not only good at but it also kept his imagination from getting away from him—most of the time—was all he wanted from life.

Well, okay, he wouldn't mind if his baseball team stopped losing so much. And he'd love to get the commission for that upcoming science fiction graphic novel. But none of that was stuff the little creature could give him. He wasn't even sure the creature could give him money or power, even if he did want it. The bribery ploy was probably just a scam.

"Come," the creature said, hands stretched toward Jaylen, palms up, sharp, black claws flicking in the track lighting as it gestured a "come here" gesture. "There must be something you want. Something you need."

"No." He needed a repaired furnace. But again, not something the little creature could help with.

It skipped forward on its four back legs, jumping close enough to make Jaylen gasp and swing out—very ineffectually—with his flashlight.

A knocking noise came from the broken furnace. Startling both Jaylen and the creature. They both turned to stare at the stack of cabinets that made up the furnace as the outer metal shivered and some pipe inside groaned.

Weird. It hadn't been making noise in months. Which was how he knew he needed to fix it. It had been cold and even relighting the pilot light hadn't got it working. The next day, he'd just found the pilot light out again. Even though he'd made excuses for the earlier noises, trying to convince himself some of those thumping sounds could come from a broken furnace, he didn't actually think the furnace would spontaneously fix itself.

So the thunking noise and metal rattling was freaking him out.

He backed upward on the stairs another step. He only noticed he'd moved upward more than once when he realized he had to bend forward a little to watch the furnace. When had he stared to move backward? Probably the minute the furnace started banging.

The banging got louder. Loud enough, even the little creature scrambled away from it.

"What's wrong with it? Is it going to explode?" the creature demanded without looking back at Jaylen.

"No, it's not going to explode." At least he hoped it wouldn't. "It's been broken. Maybe whatever was blocking it up shook loose. How do I know? Do I look like a furnace repair guy?" He barely knew how to find the buttons for restarting the pilot light. When it occurred to him the little creature might answer his question, though, he quickly added, "It's been broken for months."

"How long?" the little creature said, sounding frantic. "When? When did it break?"

"I don't know." Jaylen scowled at the back of

the creature's head, only to jump and face the noisy furnace again as the metal shivered loudly.

"Was it before or after your trip? Before or after you created the egg?"

"First, didn't create an egg. Second, I'm not sure about the timing. I don't remember checking the furnace before I left."

"But you knew it was broken after you got back?"

"I…guess. I can't remember when I noticed. Probably after the trip. No telling how long it was down before though. I can't remember."

Another loud knock, and now the furnace was trembling harder, nearly shaking out of its wall connections. That couldn't be good. In fact, that seemed like a super bad thing.

Jaylen backed up another couple steps.

Maybe it would explode. He didn't know. He didn't know the first thing about furnaces. Maybe he'd let it go too long without fixing it and it was about to punch a hole through his house.

He reined in his imagination, which was knocking at the edge of his mind, demanding he give it free run the way he had just moments ago to fix his hand. That was the problem. Sometimes, once he started using his imagination in the wrong way, it kept demanding he use it that way and wouldn't leave him alone.

The furnace bucked hard enough Jaylen thought for sure it was going to explode and started to turn to run up the stairs, little creature be damned. But he paused halfway through the turn, one foot on the higher step, when the furnace fell suddenly silent. Stopped shaking. No more thunking noise. No more noise.

Silence before the explosion? Possible. And if so, he didn't want to find out.

But when he tried to scramble up the last few stairs, his body didn't move. He couldn't take his attention from the furnace. Couldn't seem to take those last few steps. Waiting. Anticipation. Fear. Kept him rooted to the spot.

Seemed to do the same for the creature too, because it also stayed paused where it was, staring at the furnace.

Another sudden clunk. Another shiver.

And then something dark slithered out of the base of the furnace.

Chapter Five

Jaylen's heartbeat hammered so hard he couldn't hear his own panting breaths. He was barely dragging in enough oxygen to keep from passing out. Maybe not enough. He was certain he was seeing spots at the edge of his vision.

Especially because the thing rolling out of the furnace… Just. Kept. Coming.

Whatever it was, it was long. And huge. Thick. Dark. Even in the bright basement lighting with the lack of shadows, he couldn't get a good look at the thing. But it looked like a giant snake. A huge snake. Bigger than anything he'd ever even heard of or seen nature documentaries on.

And it was sliding out of his furnace!

No head yet. It seemed to be coiling around the

outside of the furnace boxes, growing thicker as it went, but he couldn't seem to *see* the head. It was lost in the slide of that huge snake-like body of darkness. There were scales. He saw those now. Everything was black though. So he only knew there were scales because some of them shimmered with a little golden purple reflection.

The furnace disappeared beneath the sliding body, the fixtures and piping pulled and tugged out of place, away from the walls. And still more of it seemed to continue wrapping around, scales sliding over scales. The noise was nails-on-chalkboard horrible, setting his teeth on edge. His scalp tingled. His base, self-preservation instincts screamed at him to run.

This was the part of the horror movie where the Too Stupid To Live character had already done the dumb thing and gone into the basement. They see the serial killer with the hatchet walking toward them. And instead of scrambling up the stairs like a normal person, they stand on the stairs, waiting for the slowly approaching serial killer while they just scream. Like that would help anyone.

To be fair, he wasn't screaming. Well, he was in his head. But no sound seemed to come out of his mouth. He only knew he was breathing because that was coming in pants that couldn't seem to drag in enough air, and he really was worried he'd pass out soon.

The creature beneath him on the stairs stared at the writhing mass of black scales wrapping around the furnace in frozen silence, too. It took a few moments, but when Jaylen realized the creature wasn't doing anything, he finally dragged his gaze away from the ginormous snake obscuring his furnace to stare at the creature.

It was transfixed. One claw tipped hand on the banister below Jaylen. One foot on the bottom step. But its entire attention was on the furnace and the snake thing. From higher on the staircase, Jaylen couldn't see the creature's expression. But it looked to be trembling.

What Jaylen wanted to say was, "We need to get the hell out of here and call animal control because that snake is big enough to eat you and me both."

What he did say was, "Hunnah hm go na."

Which probably didn't translate quite right.

The creature didn't budge. And honestly, just moments ago, Jaylen was trying to run away from the creature with its poison-tipped claws, so why he wanted to tell it to run now made no sense. Time for him to save his own ass and get the hell out of here.

Except he still couldn't move. He couldn't seem to force his feet to even change positions on the stairs, despite the clear and present danger of all the other things in the basement. That terrified heroine screaming on the stairs and *not* running away seemed a lot less implausible now. Apparently, terror did make you act like a stupid idiot who waited to get killed when running away was an option.

If he weren't about to die, he'd have had to go and apologize to all the creators who'd made horror movies with those Too Stupid To Live characters. Seems that was more of a human attribute than Jaylen ever realized.

He couldn't feel his hand gripping the banister, or the one holding the flashlight anymore. He was too afraid and his body was going numb because he couldn't force it to move. If he dropped the flashlight, he lost his only real weapon. Was that important in the face of his inability to move? Probably not.

He forced himself to blink, which was some progress. Then forced himself to look closer at the giant snake-thing surrounding his furnace. Okay. Okay. There had to be something he could do.

Even as he wondered that, something rose up from the mass of scale-covered body. Rose up over the top of the furnace near the pipes and hood thing that was supposed to feed heat back into the house. Jaylen could hear metal crunching and crinkling beneath the weight of that body. But despite the noise of impending metallic collapse, the furnace continued to support the creature.

Which was weird enough, Jaylen took a full heartbeat before he focused enough on the part that had risen above the rest of the creature to realize it was the head. A head that was not a snake's head as he'd expected.

Nope. This was a dragon's head.

Chapter Six

Jaylen thought maybe he'd died back up in the kitchen, given himself a heart attack or stroke, and was currently dying on the floor of his kitchen, surrounded by the scent of pork tacos. He was certain the doctors would assume his eating habits had gotten him in the end, not that he'd died of fright. Which was probably less traumatic for his grandmother and parents so he was okay with that cause-of-death on his death certificate.

If he was dead upstairs, that meant all this was the last grasp of his mind, the Jacob's Ladder experience right before his brain shut down completely and he shuffled off this mortal coil. But until that happened, what he was facing was absolutely terrifying and he wished, if he was already dead, that his brain would just stop already.

His brain and imagination had gotten him into enough trouble over the years. They could really stop now. That would be great.

Except nothing stopped and the head rising above his furnace still looked like a terrifying dragon's head.

Long nose like a crocodile with raised nostrils. Some tendrils like a beard but made of scales hung down from its chin. There was a ruff of hard looking spikes around the base of its head near the jaw that looked a bit like a lion's mane.

The eyes were huge, as black as its body, and only visible when it blinked translucent lids over the liquid blackness, giving it added shine in his basement's track lighting. The eyes were set on the side of the creature's head, and bulged outward underneath a heavy ridge of scales like brows.

There was another line of scales like fur down the bridge of its nose, stopping about halfway, bisecting the eyes and part of the long crocodile snout. Those scales rippled as Jaylen watched, a sort of undulating wave. Then a spiked tongue, snake-like again, slipped out of the dragon's mouth and flickered in the air.

Tasting its next meal maybe.

Jaylen could smell his own sweat and stress stink. He wondered if that would trigger the dragon-snake to attack.

Swallowing hard, he gripped the banister tighter and tried to force the thought of movement down to his feet. Even his dangerous imagination seemed to have gone quiet in the face of what he was seeing. He couldn't imagine much worse. Well, he could, probably, if his brain was working properly. But since it seemed to be shutting down, even his imagination wasn't conjuring up things to make all this worse.

He wasn't sure it could get worse.

The dragon's head bobbed one way and then the other as it lowered and turned so that it was looking at both Jaylen and the creature still standing below him at the base of the stairs.

"You…"

The sound came out slow, almost like a hiss even without the s's, and deep. Echoed through the room. And also in Jaylen's head. Like the creature had spoken both aloud and in his mind.

That sound gave him a little control of his body back. Made him blink rapidly and tightened his grip on the flashlight still somehow miraculously in his hand. That had to be progress right.

"You," the creature below Jaylen said. "It is you. But not your egg. The other. The fourteenth. You are the fourteenth egg. The hatching has begun!"

"No." The sound was deep and resonate again.

Jaylen had no idea how he was hearing a hiss

without the s's to make the sound. But he was certain that dragon was hissing when it spoke. Maybe it was the flickering tongue. Made his brain think of snake hisses and so he was inserting the sound where there couldn't be that sound.

"No?" the creature asked. "What is no?"

"The hatching has not begun. I am not yours."

"No. But you are. You are the twin. The fourteenth. I didn't know mine was a twin. We thought we'd lost you. Thought your egg gone."

"You are not the one. Not mine." The dragon's head shifted up. "He is mine."

Jaylen was really blinking now. But also panting. And seeing spots. And so confused he almost forgot his own name. "What?" he squeaked.

"You are mine," the snake-dragon said.

If by its, it meant Jaylen was its next snack, Jaylen was not okay with that.

"I don't understand," Jaylen managed to force out through his numb lips.

Suddenly a full series of images appeared in his head, like a movie, but going so fast he couldn't really "watch" it. But the knowledge of those scenes unfolded until he understood what he was seeing even if he couldn't *see* it properly.

A belching, volcanic landscape. Dark skies. No proper atmosphere. The sky above filled with the debris of a new solar system. Rocks the size of cities spinning around, some of them slamming into the landscape. Others swept away toward the inner system, more swept out to larger forming planets. No moon. Just heat and formation.

The eggs. They…gathered in these moments. No, the moments after the collision as the moon formed from the rocks strewn around the small planet, as the planet gathered more debris. As thing settled, formed. The debris swept clear. Leaving an empty orbital path. *Then*. Then the eggs…gathered.

Changes. Cooling. Oceans. Life.

The creatures, like the one on the stairs below Jaylen, came into being later. But not long after the atmosphere changed and oxygen swept the planet clean, making room for new species that could use that chemical composition. The creatures were drawn to the eggs where they were buried. Inside caves and at the base of hot springs and primitive ponds. One in an ocean. It took them awhile to find that one. And one near the base of a volcano, in one of the tubes. They could only get to that one when the lava stopped flowing.

That seemed to have taken time. A lot of time. Though all the images went through Jaylen's brain so fast, it was hard to judge the passage of time.

But a lot of time passed. The fourteenth egg… lost. No idea where it went. Thirteen remained. All cared for, coveted. Guarded. But a thread of greed there too. Hoarding them. Stealing and trading and grasping and cheating. Those who had the eggs now weren't the original guardians. They were... others.

And there was the rot of greed.

Jaylen blinked as he found himself back in his basement and only then recognized he'd not been seeing his basement surroundings for long enough that the realization terrified him. Anything could have happened. The dragon could have eaten him in those moments.

It hadn't, though. It remained where it was, wrapped around his furnace, staring at him.

He stared back. "I understand." He did. He wasn't sure how. But the knowledge was there now.

This wasn't the lost fourteenth. And yet it was. Lost...because it still had to be recreated.

The dragon turned its gaze down to the creature as the creature moved toward it.

"I am your servant, though," the creature said. "I have found you. Come for you when I knew he had you. He is not worthy of serving you."

Silence followed the creature's declaration.

Then... "No. No. I didn't do that. I was a faithful servant. I guarded the twin. I guarded my egg. He stole it. He stole it. That's why I can't find it. Why it's gone. He took it. And made you. It's not my fault!"

The last sentence was a screech of anger, rage that echoed through the basement.

For reasons Jaylen couldn't even explain, he raised his nightstick-sized flashlight in front of him, defensively, like he was going to have to use it.

The creature spun toward him. Pointed a black claw-tipped finger at him. Scrambled on its back four legs toward the stairs it had abandoned to approach the dragon. "This is his fault. All his fault."

The creature launched, so fast and suddenly, Jaylen gasped.

The dragon lunged forward.

A sharp scream cut off suddenly.

A crunch.

And the creature was gone.

Jaylen, frozen where he was, so shocked he wasn't even trembling anymore. He blinked once.

Then bent over the rail and threw up.

CHAPTER SEVEN

Darkness swirled around Jaylen. Quiet darkness that felt both comforting and terrifying at the same time. A world of warm foggy thoughts and the kind of silence he wasn't used to. His thoughts, his imagination, for once, still.

Through the silence, a voice…

Creation is your gift. And your curse.

Wasn't that an understatement. A curse. Definitely a curse. But since he made his living from that curse, he did also consider it a gift.

The fog cleared and he was at his drawing table, looking down at the piece of paper in front of him. He was supposed to come up with something for this panel. An egg. A dragon egg. And he was… reluctant to let his imagination go. He never worried about that much while he was drawing. There was this understanding that if he created on the page, *that* was the thing. The comic, the drawing, the *art* was the real thing his imagination created. The subject of the art, the thing his imagination had conjured into that art, that wasn't the real thing.

If he let his imagination run away with him while he wasn't drawing, the subject *could* become real. He thought too long and in too much depth about a thing, it happened. Something he'd first realized he could do at five when he'd desperately wanted the stuffed toy a friend of his had shown off in school. His parents wouldn't get it for him because it wasn't his birthday or Christmas. They believed presents came on important days, not just because their five-year-old wanted something. Old school parenting designed to keep from spoiling the child.

He saw their point as an adult—when he could and often did buy himself the toys he wanted whenever he wanted because it was his money now—but as a five-year-old, the lesson had not been learned yet and not getting this stuffed toy had left him in tears. He'd closed himself in his room and pictured himself holding the toy, the details of it, the feel of its soft plush against his skin, the way he'd be able to squeeze it and it would make a soft noise. So much detail, every stitch, every color. Pictured the toy in such detail he could practically feel it and smell it in his hands.

And when he'd opened his eyes, the stuffed toy *had* been in his hands. Exactly like the toy the boy at school had.

That had been the first time, but not the last. At first, he'd thought the things came from *somewhere*. That he'd pulled them from a store or something, but that they had actually existed before they showed up in his room. He was just able to bring those already existing things to him.

Then he started to accidentally create bad things. Things he knew didn't exist. The monsters from his nightmares. The hidden shadow criminals and dangers that crept into adolescent dreams. The horror show demons that were supposed to be fiction.

He'd started to draw then. After the first few times he'd conjured horrors and then had to imagine those horrors away. When he'd accepted it was his own thinking, his own thoughts, his own imagination that conjured up these things. And only his imagination could get rid of them. But getting rid of them was always much harder than coming up with them. Destroying monsters he'd built specifically from the things that terrified the shit out of him were harder to destroy when they were real and not just confined to his head. Therapy couldn't destroy the living monsters.

But in drawing them, in spilling all that imagination onto the page, he'd learned that whatever skill allowed him to bring monsters to life, recognized that creating *art* from his imagination was different. *Was* the thing, the creation. His imagination understood the difference, and if he *drew* something, that's where that something stayed. On the page. As a vibrant piece of art—that didn't walk around in the real world.

Making his living from those drawings was a bonus, and a decent living at that, but he drew to ensure his imagination had a place to go that wouldn't unleash horrors on his world.

Yet this time, this moment, when confronted with a simple task of drawing a dragon egg, Jaylen had drawn a strange sort of blank. He never got blocked. His imagination never shut up, so he always had something to draw and put on the page. Even if what he was putting on the page was just for him so he could ensure it didn't actually happen. This time, though, his imagination was strangely silent. Hesitant.

A dragon egg? Of all the things. That shouldn't have been difficult. It was just an egg after all. Maybe make it a little more alien looking than a chicken egg, of course. Bit bigger, obviously.

Rougher outer shell? Have to, right. Since this was a dragon. Maybe something metallic? Or maybe with metallic details?

He wasn't sure.

So he did what he always did when his brain needed a break. He made himself a nice meal. Did the dishes. Then he took a long, hot shower. All things designed to let his brain percolate in the background, let his imagination rest and come up with the thing he needed without him really focusing on the thing. He'd done this many times over the years. He never got blocked, but sometimes he did need a mental break so the next images could flow easier. So he could picture the thing he needed to draw next clearly instead of just moving his pencil across the page pointlessly.

When he did this, he never *thought* too hard. Didn't let his imagination go into the details. That might make the thing real. He just wanted a drawing when he was done, not whatever it was he was trying to draw. But this time, his brain latched onto the egg idea and kept at it in a way that was more… focused. While he prepared dinner, while he ate, while he cleaned up, while he showered. The image of the egg danced in his head, taking shape, growing…

It would be large, but not the size of a man, or it would have been too easy to find. Half a man's size maybe? Half his size anyway. And shaped like an oval, because people had to know it was an egg and that's what humans were used to. He couldn't draw a square egg. Readers wouldn't buy that. So an oblong oval. But larger than an ostrich egg.

The shell should definitely be different and stronger. Leather. Not metal. Scales? Some at the top and the bottom to protect those areas. But thin scales, soft scales. Not the sort of hard, impenetrable scales that would eventually cover the dragon when it emerged. He'd suggest making this one purple with green scales…

No.

Blackish leather hide with red scales and lines of purple, like veins, running over the egg's surface. Light would reflect off the dips and hollows in the leathery shell. Creating a rainbow from the dark surface, because this was fantasy after all. And there should be maybe something that looked like runes along the surface, because why not.

By the time he'd gotten into his plaid pajamas after the shower, he'd had a very clear image of the dragon egg in his head. Built with such great details, it was one of the few things he drew with color already in place. The panel he sent to the colorist had a separate sheet with the egg fully colored in, in all its details, so the colorist could get it right.

Jaylen had forgotten he'd done that. Forgotten

he'd drawn a fully detailed and shaded and colored egg.

But what he'd really forgotten was how detailed he'd *imagined* it before getting anywhere near the page to draw it. Imagined it so clearly, so distinctly…without drawing it first.

Yes… The quiet hiss in his head rolled back in with the black fog.

He floated there in that fog, the terror of what he'd done hitting him.

Do not fear creator. This was always the way.

"No." He shook his head. "No. I was supposed to draw it, not create it. I didn't mean to…"

You pictured what needed to exist. It is your purpose. And now I am here.

"Who are you?"

The fourteenth. I was to be but never came to pass. They would run riot if I was not here to balance them. But I could not…exist. When the others were set down upon this world, I was left unrealized. I needed to be realized.

"I don't understand."

The age of dragons nears. But there must be fourteen or there will be death and destruction. You needed to create me.

"You ate that creature."

He was not a true guardian. He killed the previous guardian of my twin. He was trying to bring forth the age of dragons before it was time. Before there was me.

"Is the age of dragons…now?"

Not yet, creator. Soon in cosmic time. But not so soon as for you to worry.

Good? Jaylen was pretty glad to know he wouldn't have to live through that. But, "With you, the others won't…destroy everything? Or will you all just wipe out the current species on the planet and, I don't know, rebuild from there?"

With me, we will be mighty additions to this planet. But we will not destroy it all. If it survives your species, it will survive us. So long as I was created to balance them all.

"So…I didn't unleash the end of the world on us all on accident?" That was good news. One of his greatest fears was that he'd accidentally blow up the planet with his imagination one day. Not something he could imagine a fix for like the fixes he'd had to conjure up to counter the monsters he'd created.

You have not. You have saved your planet. This world. By giving it me. Silence. Then, *And by allowing me to eat the one who would have rushed the age of dragons.*

"Yeah. That was gross."

You eat meat.

"Thanks for pointing that out. I might have to

become a vegetarian. If I wake up from…wherever this is. Am I dead?"

No.

"Dreaming?"

In a way.

"Am I imagining all this into reality?"

No. That is why we're here.

"Here? Where is here?"

In a moment, here is back in your house.

The fog began to clear again. But Jaylen clung to it a moment longer. "Wait! What now? What happens now?"

You have become a dragon guardian. Congratulations.

Jaylen wanted to argue with that last sentence, but before he could, the blackness cleared away, leaving him momentarily blinded by light.

And then he passed out cold.

Chapter Eight

Jaylen woke this time on the floor of his basement. He'd fallen down the stairs but somehow managed not to break his neck, which was surprising. The flashlight rolled along the cement floor a few feet away. He could smell his own sweat, and under that, the contents of his gut somewhere near the stairs. He narrowed his nostrils and tried not to take that smell in too easily, afraid it might make him throw up again.

Slowly, he tested his feet, legs, arms…nothing broken. Wasn't that a goddamn miracle. No idea how he could have survived the fall and not broken anything. He slowly heaved himself up to a sitting position. His head swam with the change, and his stomach lurched again. So, not completely unharmed. Probably a concussion. Damn it.

He carefully blinked in the overhead track lighting and looked around the wide open basement. His broken suitcase was up against the wall near the broken furnace, where he remembered leaving it after his last trip. The furnace sat quietly, in tact and in need of repairs he hadn't gotten around to organizing yet. The long narrow windows just below the ceiling showed only darkness from the night beyond.

It hadn't been full dark yet when he'd come down here, had it?

How long had he been unconscious? Why had he come down here again?

Everything was fuzzy. Groaning, he took his head in his hands and closed his eyes. His brain felt sluggish and slow. But at least his imagination had shut down and wasn't plaguing him with worst case scenarios. Though, maybe he should go to the hospital and have his head checked out. He'd fallen down stairs and landed on cement. He couldn't have escaped that completely uninjured, right?

He rubbed a hand over his head, not feeling any bumps or bruises. Which was really weird. Was that bad? He seemed to remember something about it being better if there was a bump. Meant the swelling was coming out instead of going inward. Brain swelling was bad, right? Yeah, maybe he should go to the hospital.

Just as soon as he could work himself up to stand.

He sure wished he could remember why he'd come down into the basement. Glancing at the broken furnace, he rubbed his hand over his neck. He really should get that fixed. Soon. He was going to need it in the winter. It was probably going to cost a fortune, though. He'd need to start saving for that now. So best to get an estimate, know what he'd have to work with.

With a deep breath, he levered himself upward, using the bottom step and then the banister to help with his balance. He expected a wave of nausea or dizziness. But outside of a moment of being off balance, by the time he stood fully, he felt fine. No dizziness or blurry vision. No nausea. Granted he was pretty sure he'd tossed up all of his dinner already…

Wait. He'd thrown up before falling. Why had he thrown up? His dinner had been fine. He didn't remember being nauseas before coming down the stairs. But to be fair, he couldn't remember coming into the basement either.

He frowned and looked around the open space. What the hell had happened?

Something clunk clunked in the furnace, drawing his attention back to it. He stared at it for a long time as something niggled at the back of his mind. Something he couldn't quite grasp. Fortunately, his imagination wasn't offering up any terrifying options, either. Which was unusual. But welcome. He was too off. If he had to worry about his imagination conjuring things right now, he wasn't sure he'd be able to stop it.

The clunk clunk from the furnace quieted. And then it made a sort of hissing noise. The sound of it coming on.

Huh. Maybe it hadn't been broken after all. Maybe something had just gotten stuck in a pipe somewhere. That would save him a fortune if he didn't have to get that fixed.

Jaylen watched the furnace for another few minutes as it quietly hummed, for the first time in a couple of months, without making strange noises.

Weird.

But he wasn't going to look a gift horse in the mouth, as his grandfather would say. Working furnace, maybe no concussion, definitely no broken bones from his fall. Everything in the basement looked normal. Guess whatever had brought him down here wasn't a big deal. Probably he just heard the furnace coming back on and it surprised him.

Yeah. That made sense. That would bring him downstairs to check on it.

He started back up the stairs, intent on getting some cleaning supplies and a mask so he could clean up his mess. Still wasn't sure why he'd thrown up, but he couldn't just leave it there. He didn't dare imagine it away. Once he started down that road, his imagination always got the best of him. Doing things by hand was always better.

He was two steps up when he remembered the flashlight and went back for it. He swept it up and then frowned at his hand. A slight tingling sensation in his skin. He flexed his fingers. Had he hurt his hand…? Couldn't remember. Didn't feel injured now. Why had he brought the flashlight down here, though? He knew for a fact the lights worked. He changed the bulbs regularly. To ensure the basement was well lit and there were no shadows. Jaylen wasn't overly fond of shadows. His imagination tended to want to turn them into scary things.

But there were no shadows. No scary things. Just a functioning furnace, and that broken suitcase he really needed to toss out.

As he started up the stairs, flashlight in hand, something dark moved just beyond his peripheral vision. A shadow that glittered like scales. Movement that made him gasp and turn quickly.

But when he looked, there was nothing there. Nothing that might have even made a shadow. Scowling, he searched the basement again, checking the corners… Nothing. Just his mess from earlier, the furnace, and the suitcase, exactly where he'd left it.

Huh.

Well, maybe he did have a concussion. He'd have to keep an eye on himself. Maybe go to the Urgent Care, just to be sure. Yeah, he'd do that. After he cleaned up the basement. Just to be safe. If he left it for overnight, there was no telling what sorts of horrible medical emergencies his brain would try to imagine up. No, better to set his mind at ease and just check it out.

He wouldn't want his imagination to get the best of him.

Lightning Through the Cats Eyes

A Destiny Cats Story

Chapter One

Erica Randal stared out across the ocean waves as wind whipped her hair back from her face. The air smelled of salt and seaweed and fish, the white caps on the restless sea bright in a dim evening sky. If the water hadn't been more purple than blue, and the sand underfoot a glistening, Pepto Bismal pink color, she could have convinced herself she was still on Earth.

There was a sun, hanging on the horizon to her left, but a red dwarf that gave the planet a strange shadowy cast. The atmosphere was perfectly fine for humans, so she could breathe and see and knew that when that red sun was higher in the sky, everything would look bright if strangely colored.

Another gush of harsh wind blew pink sand around her ankles, making her grateful for the calf high boots her aunt had made her wear—she still hadn't gotten the promised "traditional leathers" her aunt said she'd get soon, so the boots were borrowed from one of the cats. The water churned harder, waves rising high above her head but far enough out they didn't risk washing over her small group.

She could feel Galahad at her back, in his human form, close enough to pull her out of harms way if something went wrong. She never admitted it out loud, but his presence on these missions was endlessly comforting.

"What are we looking for?" she asked her aunt again, her gaze steading on the churning waves, a hand to her forehead in an attempt to block the blowing sand from getting into her eyes. Though to be fair, mostly salty sea spray hit her in the face, the heavy sand remained a tiny storm around her ankles.

"Wait," Aunt Jilly said from right beside her. "Any minute now."

Erica gave her aunt a look from the corner of her eye but kept her attention mostly on the water as directed.

Jilly was in her full guardian uniform, what she called her "traditional leathers." Leather pants, boots, loose poet's shirt that had flattened against her muscled arms in the wind, a leather vest over that, and her ever present sword, Alendrial, in the scabbard on Jilly's hip.

One day, Erica would inherit that sword. As well as Jilly's title and responsibilities. Discovering that destiny, when she'd been settling in at the history department at University of Chicago and intending on living a quiet life as a research historian, had been something of a shock.

Discovering that destiny came with a clowder of cat guards even more shocking.

Directly beside Jilly, her main cat companion, Memnon, Galahad's father, stood silently, facing the wind in his human form. The romantic relationship between Memnon and Jilly had been yet another surprise in a string of surprises, because to Erica, Jilly had always been the cool, single aunt who traveled and crafted and cursed, had too many cats, and no serious romantic relationships. A far cry from the traditional lives of her two sisters, one of which was Erica's mother.

That single status turned out to be something of a lie, but for good reason.

Memnon and Galahad bore a strong resemblance to each other in both human and cat forms. Though Memnon was obviously a lot older, his black hair threaded with silver, and a few more creases around his blue eyes. He was shorter than his son, a little shorter than Jilly, who was six foot tall, but he was thick and muscled and not the sort of warrior most smart people would mess with. He was also quite kind and patient with Erica. And once she got used to cat-Memnon also being man-Memnon, she and he had fallen into a familial, uncle-niece, relationship quite easily.

Though, to be fair, he'd known her as her a lot longer than she'd known he was anything but one of Jilly's cats.

The other five of Jilly's guard cats stood behind them, along with Erica's two additional cats. She didn't have a full clowder contingent yet. Apparently, that happened over time and the cats came to her, appearing randomly out of the cat tree now standing in the corner of her smallish apartment in Chicago when that time was right. That's how she'd met Nimue and Nester. Though, they'd all had to travel through the cat tree and into the guardian's realm for her to meet them in their human forms. In her regular, ordinary Earth realm, all of the cats had to be in cat form. Literally couldn't change to human form in that realm.

Except now that Galahad was her personal… guardian, librarian whatever, he could be a human in that realm. Just like Memnon could be human in that realm.

That had introduced some complications to the situation that Erica was still working out.

But they weren't here to worry about that. They were here to collect a book that Jilly's research had finally turned up on this watery planet under the red dwarf sun. An ancient tome that, if it fell into the wrong hands, could start a war.

Most of their job, their destiny, involved retrieving valuable books and documents and storing them safely in the temple, away from the Elders and the Wraiths and their minions. Letting either or both of those two factions get hold of the knowledge would lead to a war that could destroy all of existence in all the realms that existed.

So the job was a pretty important one.

"How long do we have to wait?" Erica asked, still trying to see what Jilly seemed to see out among the churning waves. "We've been standing here for twenty minutes."

"We've been standing here for exactly two minutes," Jilly said. "Patience. Not long now."

"You said that two minutes ago," Erica said, trying not to sigh.

The ocean was pretty and all, but the wind was cold and the sand rough when some of it did hit her skin. The waves were getting bigger too. If they started rolling toward the shore, Erica, Jilly, and the entire group were going to get washed out to sea. Erica had no idea if any of the cats could even swim. Cats weren't known for their love of water.

She glanced back briefly at her small contingent. Nimue and Nestor stood in their human forms, spread to either side and behind Galahad—who was the leader of Erica's clowder. Or well, Erica was actually the one in charge, but Galahad was their boss. Or something like that. She was still working out the pecking order.

Nimue, who was nearly as new to all this as Erica, had her hand on the sword at her hip and her lips lifted in a faint snarl. In cat form, she was a small calico with bright green eyes. In human form, she had brown and white short hair, cut loose and spikey around a pixie face with darker eyes and pale skin. She wore leathers, and had a sword, and in that moment, looked like she wanted to stab the ocean.

Erica was going to guess Nimue did not, in fact, like the water.

Nester, the older and more experienced cat, remained next to Nimue with his legs braced against the shifting beach sand and battering winds. He towered over Nimue, who was only about Erica's height. In fact, he towered over everyone, even Galahad. His long hair and beard, dark with threads of gray, blew back over his massive shoulders. Braids next to his dark temples kept that thick mass of hair back even when it wasn't windy. The creases around his green eyes were deeper as he squinted into the wind.

This was only their third adventure as a team, and Erica was still a guardian-in-training, learning how everything worked, getting to know her companions. Most of the time, when they were in Chicago, living her ordinary life, they were just the cats that hung out in her home. She talked to them—it was impossible not to talk to animals in your home—but they couldn't talk back. And so the process of really getting to know them was slow.

She liked her cohort, though. Enough that she worried about them on these adventures, even though they were better able to handle the dangers than she was. Her skills with her training sword were still…a work in progress. And they'd know their whole lives about this multi-dimensional universe.

Still, they were hers, and she tended to worry about them.

At the moment, she was worried they were getting restless and ready to move. At least Nimue looked like she wanted off the beach.

"Still waiting?" Erica asked her aunt, trying not to sound as impatient as she felt.

"Almost time." There was a sparkle in Jilly's eyes when Erica looked at her, an air of anticipation just shimmering beneath the surface.

And then, suddenly, finally, out beyond the huge waves, something crested the surface. Breaking through the whitecaps. Rising just enough to reveal a long line of spikes that fanned above the churning water before dipping back under again.

"Here he comes," Jilly murmured, the excitement in her voice obvious.

"Here who comes?" Erica's heartbeat hammered. If the spikes had been any indication—the number and size of them rising and falling beneath the surface!—whatever was out there was huge. The sort of huge that made small creatures want to scurry away and hide. Erica was a small creature compared to whatever was out there. She definitely wanted to scurry away and hide.

"You'll see. Give him a minute."

A heartbeat. The ocean churned, closer to shore now, the whitewater choppy and harsh. A rushing sound. Bubbling over the waves. And again, something breached the surface. The same spikes rose in a fan, appearing and disappearing beneath the waves. As whatever was out there got closer, those spikes were easier to see. Long as a human, sharp-tipped, silver like metal, glistening in the dim light.

Jilly gripped Erica's hand suddenly, holding tight.

And a creature rose out of the water, rising higher, and higher. So high, Erica had to drop her head back to see the thing. For a moment, all she saw were the huge, metallic silver scales. Shimmering scales moving with a crinkling sound. The water around the being sloshing back to the sea like a waterfall.

Erica blinked hard a few times, trying to get her brain to register what she was seeing. When the creature was so far above them, it was all she could see… When it was obvious if it dropped back down, it would not only cause a tidal wave, its head would land on the beach… When the head turned so that the creature was looking down at them…

That's when Erica's brain finally registered what she was looking at, finally allowed herself to really *see* what had risen above the waves.

"Is that…?" She swallowed. Knowing what she was seeing and believing what she was seeing were two very different things. "Is that a… A dragon?"

Chapter Two

Jilly laughed and shook Erica's hand, as giddy as a child on Christmas morning. Erica did not see what there was to be so excited about. This was not a laughing matter. This was not like seeing a blue whale breach from the safety of a giant ship.

This was a dragon. A dragon rising huge and silver from the purple waves. A dragon that was easily four times the size of a blue whale. And since blue whales were the largest creatures on Earth at present, that meant this dragon was four times larger than anything Erica might encounter in her world.

It was serpentine shaped, with only very stubby front legs that had webs between the digits. Along its sides were fluttering layers of fins that undulated with the being's body and created running lights along its sides. Just under the fins were two rows of blue illuminated spots that probably lit the water beneath the surface.

"It is a dragon," Jilly said, her voice as giddy and delighted as her expression. "Well, more properly a water wyrm. But yes, a dragon. Isn't he magnificent."

"Magnificent. Sure. Magnificently huge and ready to eat us!"

"Oh, he won't eat us. We don't taste good to water wyrms. Don't worry."

"That… That doesn't help."

From behind Erica, Galahad leaned forward, speaking into her ear. "The water wyrms eat the small krill-like creatures in the water. They have a baleen filter like whales on Earth. The wrym isn't any more dangerous to us than a baleen whale would be. Not even like an orca, who has teeth and would kill us if it got that into its head."

"Helpful," she muttered. And actually, it was. She wasn't an expert by a long way, but she'd been on a whale watching cruise in college and had a vague memory of the difference between baleen and teeth. "Even without teeth to eat us, that dragon is still big enough to crush us."

"Oh, it has teeth, too. In front of the layer of baleen. It just doesn't use the teeth to eat."

"I…" She had no idea what to say to that. "What does it use the teeth for?"

A suspicious beat of silence, then, "I'm not sure that will help your fear."

"What?" she squeaked and involuntarily took a step backward. She came up hard against Galahad's chest.

His hands settled on her arms, keeping her from falling in the soft, crystalline pink sand. Also keeping her from running away. Which was good. Because that would have been embarrassing to do in front of everyone.

Having his hands on her, all that heat and muscle at her back, did help distract her from the miles-high being rising above them. A little. But since that was a subject she was still grappling with, she tried to ignore the way she reacted to Galahad having his hands on her.

Really, the giant dragon looking down at them was the more important thing in that moment.

The dragon slid back into the water, leaving his head above the surface so he was more on a level with them. That didn't really help. His long, narrow head was still the size of a cruise ship, and his solid black eyes were so remarkably shark-like, Erica felt like a small, crunchy meal waiting to happen.

Thin, translucent membranes moved up and down the dragon's eyes, like he was blinking.

And then a sound like thunder erupted from the creature's mouth.

Without meaning to, Erica clamped her hands over her ears and melted farther back against Galahad. He wrapped a hand around her waist, cradling her close. Again, that created a cascade of tingles and sensations that were too complicated to think about right then, but also went a long way toward distracting her. She wasn't sure he was doing that on purpose. But those jolts of...reaction were pulling her back from the brink of panicked screaming, so at least on that level, the sensations were helpful.

Jilly dipped into a low bow from the waist, her head down. Erica felt the panic rising again, seeing her aunt that vulnerable. But the dragon didn't attack. Instead, he dipped his head a bit under the water, as if returning the bow.

Okay. So. Erica let out a breath. Jilly obviously knew what she was doing. And Erica trusted her aunt. Jilly had been doing this destined guardian job for a very long time. The sheer terror of facing a creature that huge was completely understandable, but if Jilly wasn't afraid, was in fact delighted, then obviously this wasn't as terrifying a situation as it appeared on the surface.

"The wyrm is here to help," Galahad said against her ear.

His warm breath and equally warm body at her back were reassuring and comforting, but also made her entirely too aware of her body. "Help with what?"

"Getting to the book we're here to retrieve."

That… What?

Jilly pulled Alendrial from her scabbard in that moment and held the sword up in front of her. The move had Erica widening her eyes and flicking her gaze between the wyrm and her aunt. A drawn sword seemed like a threat. Except the way Jilly held the sword in front of her face, point up at the sky looked more like a solute.

"Great and powerful Wyrm," Jilly said. "Thank you for seeing us."

A sound from the wyrm seemed to vibrate on the air, a much softer sound than the one that had made Erica cover her ears moments before. There were actually visible currents in the air from the sound, like a shimmering of damp wind. That shimmering hit the sword and a voice said, "It is an honor to assist you. What do you seek, Guardian?"

Oh. Wow. Did… "Did Alendrial just translate what the wyrm said?"

"She did," Galahad said. "One of the swords many uses. She's not just a weapon."

Erica had known that on some level. Alendrial was also the key into the sacred temple were all the books and documents they retrieved for safe keeping were stored. But it had never occurred to her that Alendrial could do so much more than fight and open the temple.

She had questions for her aunt when they got back.

"We seek the ancient Book of Time, hidden this many eons from the Wraiths and Elders."

As Erica watched a visible shimmering vibration from Alendrial traveled across the beach and space of ocean between Jilly and the wrym, melting against the wyrm as it reached the creature.

The fins alongside the creature's neck, the only ones above water that Erica could see anymore, fluttered in that vibration. And then another movement of visibly shimmering air from the wyrm back to Jilly and Alendrial.

"The wrym speaks in…vibrations?" Erica murmured to Galahad, hoping the sound she made didn't disrupt the sound wave from the wrym.

Galahad nodded, his hair brushing her temple. "We all do, of course. Sound vibrations translated through our ears. But the wyrm's vocabulary is a bit difficult, and their language hard for humans to even hear."

Erica was starting to wonder if she'd better brush up on her basic biology for this job.

From Alendrial, "The Book of Time is one of many. It cannot be used without the others."

"We are still searching for the others," Jilly said through the sword, "so that they may be safeguarded in the temple. We do not believe the Wraiths or Elders have found them. Yet."

"You believe they are close."

"We do. Which is why it is time to retrieve the book whose location we do know."

"It has been safe here for many ages," the wyrm said.

"Yes. But it will not be much longer. It is time to move it to the temple. It is time." Jilly smiled behind Alendrial, as if she'd just made a joke. But her expression grew more serious, her tone somber as she said, "We would not want the attention of the Wraiths or the Elders to fall upon your world."

The wyrm held still as the churning water around it slapped against its metallic scales. Even the fins along its neck stilled.

Finally, it said, "We would not. But traveling to the depths is dangerous for your species. And that of your guard."

"Which is why we are here seeking your help, oh Great One."

A sound like a chuckle from the wyrm itself, not translated through Alendrial. Though why Erica thought that hum of vibrating air sounded like a chuckle she wasn't sure.

"Flattery. I am not an Elder god," the wyrm said through Alendrial.

"Close, though. Just without the realm-destroying ambitions."

Jilly's comment had Erica wondering just how old the wyrm was. The implied age was… mindboggling.

"I would live in peace with the other realms," the wyrm allowed. "But when you are one of only a dozen of your species, peace is…necessary."

"It is. I would safeguard your peace now, by removing a reason for the higher gods to come looking for you."

A rumbling sound, almost like thunder, and the fins along the wyrm's neck trembled. "I will take you to that which you seek."

In the next instant, the wyrm dropped below the water, so fast the move left a hole in the ocean surface that filled in like a waterfall dropping into a pool.

Erica blinked. "I…I thought it was going to help."

"It is," Jilly said. "Don't worry." She resheathed Alendrial and looked around. "We'd better wait farther up the beach."

"For what? What are we waiting for?" Erica hurried after Jilly and Memnon, though that meant Galahad had to release her and that was… disappointing. The disappointment was complicated so she pushed that aside for now. "What's happening?"

"The Book of Time has been on this planet, in this realm, for eons," Jilly explained as they stopped by the cat tree that had brought them to this world. It sat near the solid pink rocky cliffs that ran behind the beach, rising almost as tall as the wrym had been when it rose out of the water.

Sometimes the cat trees were exactly like a carpet-covered cat trees on Earth, a place for small cats to climb and claw and hid inside boxes so as not to be disturbed by their human. Most of the destiny cat trees were huge, but they grew as the situation called. Jilly had a giant cat tree taking up half her bedroom because she had a full cohort of guards. Erica's cat tree was still a relatively moderate sized tree because she only had three guards so far. Jilly assured her that tree would continue to grow. Erica would have to get a bigger apartment if it got too much bigger.

Some of the trees at exits, like this world, were not those artificial trees covered in carpet and fur, but actual real trees. She'd exited into new worlds through palm trees, through giant oak trees, through the huge, oversized spruce trees that populated the forest outside the temple.

The tree in this world was the most unique thing she'd seen so far. It reminded her of a cross between a cactus, a tumbleweed, and seaweed. Only huge. Spreading vine-like into the sky but without actually attaching to the cliff face. A deep purple color, with hints of blues, the "tree" even smelled a bit like seaweed—that salty, briny, fishy scent—but softened and not too strong. At least to her. She did wonder what the cats smelled since they had a better sense of smell than she did. But also, cats—hers anyway—liked fish, so it probably smelled good.

"So, I got the part about the book being here for a long time," Erica said, her gaze jumping between Jilly and the rolling ocean waves. "And I assume from that conversation that the wyrm has been guarding it?"

"Yes. For a very long time. And until recently, that was a secret. Only the guardians have passed that information down. It was felt the book was safest here, rather than bringing attention to its existence."

"There are more like it? A bunch of them?"

"Twelve all together. And no one individual book has much power. But when combined... When combined the Book of Time is extremely dangerous. Especially in the hands of the Wraiths or Elders."

"Are the others guarded by other wyrms?" The wrym had said it was one of only a dozen members of its species. Those numbers matched up very neatly. And Erica was coming to realize there were very few coincidences in the Universe.

Jilly's gaze jumped to the sea. "We'll have to discuss that once we return to the temple. It's time to go."

"Go where?"

"To the bottom of the sea."

"Wait. What?" Erica looked out at the huge waves, the white caps churning as the wind whipped across the surface. "You got a submarine around here I don't know about?"

Jilly was grinning when Erica faced her again. "Of a sort."

Erica frowned. "You're having way too much fun with all this."

"I enjoy my work."

Memnon chuckled quietly. The chuckle was not a reassuring sound.

"It'll be fine," Galahad said.

"You've done this before?"

"Once. It's been a while, though." He glanced out at the waves. "Not a great swimmer."

"I'm an excellent swimmer," Nimue said suddenly into the sound of crashing waves. But she looked nervously out at the ocean, too. "In a pool."

"You've swum? In a pool?" The way Nimue had been glowering at the sea earlier, Erica would have laid money that the younger cat hated water and getting wet. Learning she could swim was quite enlightening.

Erica's fascination stuttered to the back of her mind, though, when the churning, seething ocean caught her full and undivided attention. The whitecaps looked like foam, the purplish water rising and falling in huge waves.

Erica expected the wyrm to rise out of the sea again. Instead, something roughly the shape of a missile shot out of the water, arched high overhead, and dropped with an ominous whistle to the beach.

Chapter Three

Instinctively, Erica leapt backward, hitting up against one of the branches of the seaweed tree. Galahad caught her before she fell—or went through the tree, back to the temple!—and held her by the arm until she got her feet under her.

The missile hit the sand with a thud, sending pink crystals up in a dense puff. When the sand settled, a long, narrow, silver spike stuck out of the sand.

A spike that looked suspiciously like one of the spikes that had lined the wyrm's back.

"Did the wrym just try to kill us with a spike?" Erica asked, staring at the glistening weapon.

"Of course not." Jilly snorted.

Erica opened her mouth, and two more spikes shot into the air, arched high overhead, and dropped to the beach within feet of the first one, a neat precision row that shouldn't have been possible when the wrym's head wasn't even out of the water to see its shots.

"You sure about that?" Erica asked. "Because it's shooting very sharp missiles at us."

"Not *at* us. *For* us."

Erica gave her aunt a look.

Jilly gave in with a huff. "Why do you have to ruin my fun?"

"This isn't fun. Give. What's with the spikes?"

"They're our submarines. So to speak. Pressurized vessels that will get us to where we're going. The cavern has some breathable air trapped in it. Or it did the last time we were here. We'll be safe once we're inside. Hopefully. But getting there requires—"

Erica held up a hand to interrupt her aunt. "Maybe, probably, hopefully. Those are not reassuring words, Aunt Jilly."

"Always some risk," Jilly said with a shrug.

Erica hadn't had "crushed under the pressure of an alien sea," or "choked to death in undersea cavern due to no oxygen" on her death bingo card. She supposed she should upgrade that card now that she was a Temple Guardian in training.

"Come along." Jilly marched toward the row of spikes. "You're going to love the inside of these."

Erica trotted to keep up, her feet sinking into the pink crystalline sand. "Inside? What's inside?"

Jilly shook her head. "You'll see soon enough. Why ask when you can see with your own eyes?"

"You've been hedging and feeding out information very slowly so far. I'm trying to get ahead of the situation so I stop feeling so far behind."

"Well, when you put it that way." Jilly sighed. "The inside of the spikes are hollow and will fill with plenty of breathable air when we climb inside."

"Why only three?" But as they approached the spikes, Erica got that answer for herself.

The things were huge. A lot bigger than they'd looked on the wyrm or launching out of the sea. As thick around as an elevator and almost as tall as the cliffs behind them. There wouldn't be room inside one for their entire group unless the spikes had something like different levels in all that height. But there was definitely room across the three spikes for all eleven of them.

The shimmer of silver that looked like metal seemed even more like metal up close. In fact, the closer she got, the more the spikes looked like something *built* rather than something biologically grown on a living creature.

"How do we get inside?" she asked, but quietly, as she frowned at the smooth surface of one spike.

Jilly tapped something along the center of the spike, and a seam opened up the length, like a zipper unzipping, but the noise it made was like a sword sliding out of a scabbard. And a little ting sound from the metal actually shivered the sand under it.

More vibrations.

The other two spikes followed moments after the first, sliding open with a metal-on-metal sound. No one had even touched the other two, though.

"How?" Erica seemed to be asking that a lot.

"They're linked," Jilly said. "They'll do the same thing most of the time."

"So...if one fails underwater and breaks up, killing everyone inside, the other two will do the same thing?"

"Such a pessimist. Trust the wrym. We'll be fine."

Erica opened her mouth to ask more how and what questions, but finally decided to take Jilly's advice and just wait for it. The answers she was getting now were making her anxiety climb rather than settling her nerves.

Galahad leaned in again and whispered, "They spikes won't rupture. The deeper they go into the water, the stronger they are."

"Then how do we get out of them in these underwater caverns?"

"Same way we get into them. But they need to be out of the water for that to happen."

"In the cavern?"

"In the cavern."

"Isn't the pressure in the cavern going to kill us?"

"It's a protected space. I've been there and I didn't die. We'll be fine."

"Reassuring."

"You don't sound reassured."

"Hey, you really are getting to know me." She was half joking, but the joke touched on all those awkward issues they'd both been avoiding and made her cheeks heat. She kept her focus on the spikes and hoped he didn't notice, getting back to the subject at hand. "Is this technology or biology?" The spikes looked so very much like metal it was hard to tell.

"Both!" Jilly said from the entrance to one spike. "Isn't it wonderful."

"Still having way too much fun," Erica called.

Jilly laughed.

"Is she drunk?" Erica murmured to Galahad.

"She's a bit of an adventure junky."

Erica found herself chuckling despite her nerves.

When she finally looked back, Galahad was smiling. That changed the nervous jumping in her stomach yet again. He didn't smile often. She very much liked when he did.

"Let's get moving," Jilly called. "You and Galahad in one. Me and Memnon in another. Nester, you look after the younglings."

Several of Jilly's cats snorted at that. Nimue blushed. In the end Memnon sorted everyone out between the three spikes so that there were four people in each of two spikes and three in the last spike.

As Erica watched everyone move toward their different spikes, she said, "Couldn't you all just…go cat and then we could travel together? This feels unsafe, splitting up."

Jilly stalked up to her and held her by the shoulders, making her meet her aunt's gaze. "These are a very safe mode of transportation. You ride the El regularly. It is significantly less safe than these spikes. You will be fine. We will all be fine." She leaned in. "There's magic *and* technology involved. If you can't trust the technology, can you trust the magic?"

For some reason, which was completely illogical for a woman who only discovered there *was* magic less than a year ago, she sort of trusted the magic more.

And wasn't that something she was going to

have to discuss with a therapist. Except she couldn't talk about any of this with a therapist.

"So my choices are a strange sort of alien dragon technology that is also biology, or just trust magic?" she asked, just to be clear.

"Those are your choices, yes."

"Abracadabra and hocus pocus, then, I guess."

Jilly laughed and gave her a hug. "You're going to love the cavern. Just wait. Talk about magical!"

"You are drunk, aren't you?"

Jilly waved a hand in the air, which wasn't really a denial, as she hurried back to Memnon.

Erica took once last look at the huge rolling purple ocean, the pink cliffs and crystalline sand. Watched as the others all entered their respective spikes without all the waffling. Even Nimue jumped into the spike, her eyes wide with curiosity.

Galahad waited for Erica, remaining at her side as she carefully looked into the spike. Nimue and one of Jilly's cats, Morgaine, were already inside. Memnon hovered half inside his spike, waiting on Erica and Galahad to climb in.

She was holding everyone up, but this was one of the more terrifying things she'd ever done, and that included going into a desert chasing after all the cats because they'd been caught by a spell.

"It's okay to be scared," Galahad said.

"Nimue isn't scared."

"I am," Nimue called. "But also excited. They are very similar feelings."

"There you go," Galahad said. "Pretend all that fear is excitement."

"Right. That's what this is." She pulled in a deep breath. She hadn't seen any sign of the wrym since the spike shit the beach. Which begged one last question. "How do these get back into the water to the wrym?"

"Have you been on a rollercoaster before?" Galahad asked.

"Long time ago. When I was a teenager."

"Did you love it or hate it?"

"Loved it. Hated the Ferris wheel. Too slow. Very scary."

"You preferred the speed of the rollercoaster?"

"I guess you could put it that way." She nodded.

"Good. Then you'll love this."

She widened her eyes. "Have you been on a rollercoaster?"

"No."

"Then how do you know that's what will happen?"

"I've seen the YouTubes. And those are a great approximation of what this will feel like. At least until the spikes reconnect with the wyrm."

"If I throw up, I'm blaming Jilly," she muttered. And finally climbed into the spike.

The interior was just a cylindrical open space, the same silver metallic color as the exterior of the spike. When she touched the wall, it was cool and slick but not slimy or wet. In fact, it felt a little like pearl even though it looked like metal. She ran her fingers over the wall, wondering which was the closer analogy, metal or pearl. Whichever it was, it lit up with a florescent blue light along the path of her fingers.

The entire interior of spike was actually illuminated by the walls, a soft sort of white-blue colored light that was fainter than the bright blue that ran over the surface under her touch.

Above her head, the spike continued up and up and up to a point. A long way up. When she remembered the trajectory of the spike, it occurred to her that they could all end up in the roof of this thing. Then she looked down and realized she was standing on thin air.

Or rather, she was standing on something that felt solid, but she could see between her feet to the bottom of the spike. She sort of wished that part wasn't so well lit, even though it was dim, because this reminded her too much of being on a Ferris wheel, being able to look down between her feet.

She dragged her gaze back up quickly, afraid the

view would give her vertigo, and looked around for a seat, or something to hold on to. The wall seemed to be the only thing to brace against. Galahad, as if reading her mind, pressed a hand flat against the wall, and a series of handholds popped out as well as what looked like clamps from the see-through floor.

"What are those?" She nodded down at the clamps.

"You put your feet in those. They seal over and hold you in place when we need to be held in place."

"So…we just clamp our feet in and hold on for dear life?"

"The hand holds become like a harness. They'll keep us safe until we don't need them anymore."

"Do I want more details about that?"

"Probably not until after it happens."

She opened her mouth to argue, but the spike sealed shut in that moment and that meant something was going to happen soon and she didn't want to be hanging out in all that open space when it did and end up jammed into the point of the spike.

Galahad waited until she had her feet clamped into place and was leaning between two of the handles, before he clamped his feet in. What had looked like handholds then folded out and wrapped around her and Galahad almost like arms, or, as he'd said, like a seatbelt harness, only it locked her arms close to her sides as well.

That part was a little unnerving, so she tried not to focus on it. It was better than flailing around the interior when whatever was about to happen... happened.

She glanced across the narrow spike to see Nimue staring with wide eyes at the harness wrapping around her and Morgaine giving Galahad a speculative look.

Morgaine grinned and to Erica said, "If it makes you feel better, Galahad threw up the first time we did this. You throw up, you'll be in good company."

Galahad scowled his former guardian cat companion. She just laughed, unrepentant.

The banter—and hearing Galahad hadn't been so sanguine the first time he'd done this either—actually did help. Made her feel less like a scared idiot.

And now that she felt secured and not likely to go flying around, and she wasn't looking down between her feet, this did feel more like a rollercoaster. That made her adrenaline spike in a good way. She actually was starting to feel the excitement. While she might not be quite the adrenaline junky that her aunt was, she had been looking forward to all the adventures this destiny afforded her. And this was going to be one hell of an adventure.

That kernel of excitement, that stirring of acceptance and curiosity…

Turned into a scream of terror when the spike suddenly shot straight up into the air.

Chapter Four

Erica would have slapped a hand over her mouth if she'd been able to move her arms, both embarrassed by the scream and also a little afraid she really would throw up. The spike rocketed straight up, paused, and then started falling back toward the ground. The harness kept her snug and secure against the wall, without even enough give to worry the harness might break. She felt the pressure of the fall, and her stomach shot up to her throat as they seemed to be dropping head first back toward the ocean. But she didn't wiggle around within the security harness even a little.

She heard Morgaine laugh. And Nimue actually whooped. And even Galahad chuckled.

Everyone having a grand old time as she fought

to keep her breakfast down. She was surrounded by adrenaline junkies.

Keeping her lips clamped shut so she'd neither scream again nor risk tossing up her cookies, she squeezed her eyes nearly closed and waited for the cataclysmic crash when they hit the ocean.

A cataclysmic hit that…never happened.

Instead, they slowed at a pace that defied gravity, and eventually just stopped falling. Or at least it felt like they'd stopped falling. Erica opened her eyes and looked around.

A sound like a ca-chunk-chunk. A vibration up through the spike at her back. And then everything stilled.

The cats all sighed and grinned and seemed wholly satisfied with what had just happened. Erica looked at Nimue. "Have you done this before?"

"No. But I've heard about it. If this is what riding a rollercoaster in your realm is like, I'm sorry I can't ride them."

Yeah, Erica was pretty sure no one in her realm would let her take a cat on a rollercoaster. "It's…" She thought about it a moment, then shrugged. Or tried to around the securely fitted harness. "It actually was a little like that. With less jerking sideways and fewer ups and downs than a rollercoaster. But the drop… Yeah, that was pretty rollercoaster-ish."

And now that they'd landed safely—wherever that was—and it was all over, in hindsight, Erica realized the stomach dropping descent had actually been pretty fun. Damn. If she'd known the landing was going to be so soft, she might even have tried to enjoy that part more.

"Where are we now?" She turned to Galahad, who was smiling softly. It was a good look on him, that soft smile. But probably not good for her concentration.

He blinked at her and said, "We've reattached to the wyrm. Give it a minute, and you'll be able to see everything."

"Wait." She scanned the interior of the spike. "We're...*on* the wrym now?"

"Yes, where did you think we'd go?"

"I don't know. Maybe we'd land in the water and it would...drag us down or something?"

"It does have to drag us to the bottom. With all this air inside the three spikes, it's very buoyant now. It will take a lot of muscle to get us to the bottom."

For some reason that was reassuring, that the spikes were buoyant at the moment.

"So are we...reattached to the wrym's spine?"

"We are."

Erica looked down through her feet to the dimly lit bottom of the spike. From the inside, it didn't look any different than it had when it was imbedded in the sand. "That's actually pretty cool," she murmured.

"Jilly said we'd enjoy this part," Nimue said.

She was grinning a lot. It was probably the most Erica had ever seen her smile. Though Nimue did smile easily when in human form. It was just that Erica had never seen her grin with such excitement.

Morgaine, whose smile was no less enthusiastic than Nimue's, said, "Wait until you see this next part."

Nimue's green eyes widened. She looked across the spike to Erica and said, "I'm so glad we get to do this! Thank you."

"Why are you thanking me? Jilly is the one who brought us here."

"Because you let me be your guard, I get to have this adventure. So thank you."

Erica swallowed and flicked a quick glance at Galahad. She wasn't sure how to answer that. Because she hadn't realized she had a say in who her guard cats were. They were just supposed to show up, right? That's what she understood. And then they all settled in to develop a group that would, eventually—hopefully a long time from now—replace Jilly and her cats as the guardians of the temple and bookkeepers and all that. No one had mentioned to Erica that she might…reject one of the cats.

Not that she would with either Nimue or Nester. She quite liked both of them. And as for Galahad…

She had no idea if she had a choice in him being her…whatever he was. She supposed librarian was one of his titles. But the way everyone had talked, it was just a foregone conclusion that he would replace his father as the temple librarian and personal guard to the next temple guardian. And that the next temple guardian would be Erica because of a family legacy.

No one had mentioned Erica had a *choice* in which cats made up her personal destiny cat clowder.

From the way Galahad avoided her gaze, she wondered if that hadn't been on purpose. If all of them, Jilly included, had failed to mention the choice for a specific reason.

After this adventure, she intended on asking her aunt what that reason might be.

But even as she wanted the answers, she knew the explanation wouldn't change anything on a practical level. Nimue and Nester were *her* cats now. She wanted to keep them. And Galahad…

Well, even with the complication of the things they didn't talk about, she still wanted to keep him too.

Another series of vaguely ca-chunk sounds and them movement waved up through the spike. She felt the vibration at her back and through the harness, like a full body massage happening all at the exact same time. It felt good, that vibration, which was another surprise. A lot of surprises happening on this adventure.

A moment after the vibration wave, the spike moved, a kind of undulation that made Erica's stomach roll, but in a good rollercoaster way, and then the harnesses and foot clamps released and melted back into the walls and see-through floor.

Erica blinked down and around as she eased away from the support of the wall. "What's happening now?"

"Wait," Galahad said, his voice quite and deep. "Watch the walls."

A little afraid to move around too much in the narrow space and knock into the others, Erica turned in place to stare at the wall. For a heartbeat, nothing happened.

And then, the wall she'd thought was either metal or pearl started to shimmer. Suddenly, everything got dark, so dark she reached instinctively for Galahad. He was there, grabbing her hand unerringly, giving her fingers a gentle squeeze of reassurance.

Then rapid blue lights, the same color as the

lights under the dragon's fins, started racing up and down the length of the spike. Turning the interior of the space a bright blue that was both brighter and dimmer than it had been a moment ago. The effect reminded her of being at a show or in a night club were the overhead lights go out, but the spotlights swing around, casting bright circles of light in smaller areas.

As she watched the lightshow, she heard Nimue gasp and turned to check on her. Then gasped herself. The wall in front of Nimue seemed to be disappearing.

Erica backed into Galahad. "What's happening?" The panic in her voice was only a little embarrassing.

"It's not breaking," he said against her temple. "See? The barrier is still there."

Nimue pressed the space where the wall had been, still a solid surface. Just translucent now. Nimue looked back at Erica and grinned. "It feels like glass now."

"Sturdy glass?" Erica asked as she eased away from Galahad to touch the wall next to Nimue. "Sturdy glass!" The wall felt as solid as it had a few moments ago, even when she pressed hard against it.

It was just no longer opaque.

"Holy shit," she murmured. Then she looked

outside the glass. And found herself backing up into Galahad again. "Whoa."

The dark purple waters of the sea streamed past. No longer whitecapped waves, but deeper, and darker. Not even the dim red sun reaching to this depth.

But despite the water's darkness—or really probably because of that—the ocean was filled with bright spots of light. Bioluminescent creatures of all shapes and sizes bobbed past, from the tiniest specks of pink light, to larger jellyfish-like creatures in rainbow-colored hues.

"Wow."

That was the best she could do. She'd never seen anything like the scene outside the transparent spike. Not even at an aquarium. Which, she supposed made sense since none of these were earth creatures. The shapes were much less symmetrical, with odd angles. Many of them were flattened, but others were bulbous, some contained essentially translucent "skins" while others had carapaces or outer shells.

And all of them were lit from within. A bright, rainbow cacophony of personalized illumination.

"Beautiful, isn't it?" Galahad murmured.

"Beautiful." She looked up at him and smiled. Then realized the rest of the spike was now translucent too. The entire thing. She could see down to the wrym's back, up to where the surface of the ocean probably was above them, out all of the different angles to different parts of the ocean. They were now riding in a completely see-through biological submarine.

"Uhm, can the other creatures out there see us? Like, will they…attack because we look like food?"

Not that anything she'd seen so far was larger than the wyrm. In fact, nothing out there looked like it even had teeth. Still, that didn't seem like something she'd want to take for granted on an alien planet in a different realm.

"Nothing would dare attack the wrym," Galahad said, "even if the strange things inside its spine spikes looked like food. Which we don't. To most of the beings here, we look like…part of the spikes. Maybe parasites? Or they just can't see us because they don't have those kinds of perceptions. They'd be more likely to 'hear' us, our sound vibrating out of the spike and through the water. But even then, we won't sound like food."

"This is wild," she breathed, standing in the very center of the spike so she could see all around.

Nimue joined her in that spot, and they stood back to back circling to take in the full panorama view. Morgaine grinned, her gaze jumping between Erica and Nimue, and the scene outside the walls.

Whenever Erica glanced his way, Galahad's

attention was on her. His expression was soft and thoughtful. Not smiling, which was a shame. But like he was contemplating something.

She wanted to ask what he was thinking, but this seemed like a bad time.

"How deep are we going?" she asked instead. "I mean, I know it's the bottom of the ocean here, but how deep is that, exactly?"

"Not quite as deep as the average ocean depth on Earth," he said, with a shrug.

"That's still not an answer."

"The number sounds big. It might make you more nervous when you don't have to be."

"Galahad."

Nimue's eyebrows shot up at Erica's warning tone, but she kept her attention on the passing bioluminescent show. Morgaine made a quiet sound that was hard to interpret when Erica couldn't see her face.

She was too busy holding Galahad's gaze, making sure *he* knew she wasn't going to put up with any more prevaricating. She'd had more than enough of that on the beach, thank you very much. More than enough of the muddying of information or just leaving things out for dramatic effect. Right now, she just wanted a straight answer.

He let out a resigned sigh and said, "About three thousand meters."

"Thank you!" He was right. Three thousand meters was very deep and a very big number. But less spooky than hearing it said in feet, which she appreciated. And she worked hard to ignore the translation of that number to feet in her head even though her brain was currently screaming *that's nearly TEN thousand feet! Ten THOUSAND feet!*

Three thousand meters didn't sound too bad in comparison. So long as she refrained from comparing that number to Galahad's height. He was less than two meters tall. It would take more than fifteen hundred Galahads to reach the bottom of the ocean. Closer to sixteen hundred Galahads.

That was a lot of Galahads.

She gave her head a little shake. Those thoughts were *not* helping. And she didn't want to prove Galahad right by freaking out about the big number after insisting he tell her.

To redirect her brain from the fact that they were going to a part of the ocean that could absolutely crush her instantly if this spike didn't hold out, she went back to studying the myriad animals outside.

That triggered awe rather than fear. Just... "Amazing," she said when something larger than anything they'd seen so far swam past. It was still sort of jellyfish shaped, but huge compared to the other beings, and rounder and flatter at the same time, and translucent with rows of green and yellow luminescent lights running up and down its length.

The creature followed along side them for quite a ways, eventually drawing a frown from Galahad.

That frown had Erica right back to worrying, a feeling she'd been able to dump for exactly one minute and twenty-three seconds. "What?" she asked.

"Nothing. Just…"

"You don't finish that sentence, and I'm going to start throwing around glares and getting huffy."

This statement turned his frown into almost a smile. And Nimue covered her mouth to hide a laugh. Obviously unsuccessfully since Erica was perfectly aware she was chuckling.

Morgaine, on the other hand, had moved up closer to the wall on the side of the wrym with the larger creature keeping pace with them, and she was also frowning at it.

"It's going to try eating us, isn't it?" Erica asked, when she noticed Morgaine's expression.

"No," Galahad said. "But…it doesn't belong here. It's not *of* this ocean."

Erica's turn to frown. "It looks just like everything else here." Sort of. It was bigger. But there was a creature in this ocean the size of the wyrm they were riding. There had to be big things moving around here, right? "Is it it's size?"

"It's the color and shape of its luminescent cells. They're wrong for this part of the ocean."

"It's supposed to look like it belongs," Morgaine murmured. "To someone not paying attention. Or someone who wouldn't know better."

"You know better," Erica said.

"We've been here before."

Galahad moved up next to Morgaine, both of them studying the creature now. Nimue joined them, her gaze jumping between the two more experienced cats and the creature outside. Because the space inside the spike wasn't all that large, this repositioning of everyone moved Erica back closer to the other wall, and also served as a buffer between her and the anomalous creature. She was pretty sure the cats weren't doing that on purpose, but not entirely certain because they were her guards after all.

"Is it dangerous?" she asked.

The creature moved as fast through the water as the wyrm and it was that realization that really clicked for Erica. None of the other creatures moved that fast. They either just floated on the currents or bounced forward in little puffs of movement. Nothing *swam* the way the wyrm was swimming. And while Erica assumed there were things in this ocean that swam, she knew they hadn't seen any here, in this part of the ocean, at this depth.

But this flat, green and yellow creature was keeping pace with the wrym, swimming through the other bioluminescent beings like they were dust motes. It was also remaining at the same distance from the wyrm, neither floating too close or too far away.

She couldn't see anything inside its transparent skin, the way it could probably see them inside the wyrm's spine spike. But for some reason, that didn't help Erica's jumping nerves.

In fact, her heartbeat was picking up speed the longer that creature kept pace with them.

She also noticed no one had answered her question about whether it was dangerous or not.

Tempted to ask it again, she glanced over her shoulder. And spotted a second of the larger green and yellow creatures. Keeping pace with the wyrm.

"We've got two of them," she said, staring at the newest creature.

Galahad moved up to her side, cursed—which she didn't hear him do often—and stalked to the part of the spike facing the front of the dragon.

He pulled his sword from the scabbard at his hip. No one had a sword like Alendrial. Everyone else just carried run of the mill swords. But it was still a sword, made of metal and kept bright and shiny and sharpened.

"You're not going to...cut anything, right?"

Erica wasn't sure why she'd asked. Just seeing his sword out in such a tight space was unnerving. But the entire situation was unnerving so…

He held the sword point up and angled it this way and that until she realized he was catching light on its surface. The blue light that suffused the transparent wall of the spike. After a moment of staring at him and watching, she glanced out the wall, in the direction he was looking, and spotted a flickering of blue light from one of the spikes farther along the wyrm's back.

The others! She'd nearly forgotten about everyone else, in their own spikes, arrayed along the wyrm's back. She hadn't seen them in the darkness, but apparently their spikes were now transparent too, because the light coming from that other spike was definitely flickering and moving in ways light didn't naturally move.

She watched in fascination, trying not to dance from foot to foot in her impatience, her gaze occasionally flicking to the two large creatures bracketing them in.

Finally, Galahad lowered his sword and cursed again. When he faced them all, he looked grim.

"I was afraid of this," he muttered. Then looked Erica in the eyes and said, "The Elder-sworn have found us."

Chapter Five

When Jilly had first introduced Erica to her destiny as a temple guardian, they'd been running away from Wraith-sworn, creatures who served the Wraiths and who were trying to invade the temple and get at all the knowledge the guardians had been safeguarding for eons, across multiple realms.

This had been bad.

Her only real memory of the Wraith-sworn was as shadowy figures darkening the bright sky and filling her with dread as she and the cats and Jilly had raced toward the temple. There'd been a fight, but she'd been focused on other things at the time, so hadn't even gotten a good look at them.

She hadn't encountered an Elder-sworn yet, not in all the months she'd been training, not in any of her first few adventures to reclaim lost books. In fact, she hadn't thought much about what an Elder-sworn would be.

She was thinking about it hard now.

"Are you telling me Elder-sworn are… bioluminescent sea creatures?" she asked, pretty sure she already knew the answer was *no*, but just in cast… "That seems pretty limiting."

"They can take many forms," Galahad said. "That's part of the problem with the Elder-sworn. They can blend in better than their counterparts. And the Wraith-sworn would have a difficult time reaching beneath the sea here without help. Like their masters they're more…ephemeral."

"I remember," she muttered. "But not so ephemeral that they can't leave cuts and wounds and even kill."

Morgaine winced at that, and Erica had to wonder why.

"It doesn't matter which it is, Wraith-sworn or Elder-sworn," Galahad said. "The fact is that one group has found us and we're not going to be able to just collect the book now."

"We can't exactly fight them like this," Nimue pointed out.

She didn't *sound* panicked. But Erica still heard a little edge under her words. Erica had no idea if Nimue had actually faced any of the creatures serving the Wraiths and Elders before. She was new to the destiny cats, but that didn't necessarily mean she was new to this fight. And also, as a guardian, it was officially her job to ensure Erica's safety. That part of the job had just kicked up a notch.

"Not without risking the wrym's life," Galahad said.

"What? They can hurt the wrym?" Erica looked out the wall at one of the creatures pretending to be an ordinary sea animal. It was much larger than anything else they'd seen, but it was still smaller than the wrym by a lot. It didn't even take up the length of two spine spikes along the wyrm's back. "Couldn't the wrym just slap them with its tail and be done with it?"

"These being serve the Elders. Their appearance is deceptive. You can't judge their danger by whatever form they choose to take. Remember, they've picked this form to blend in rather than to fight."

"Can they change shapes quickly, easily?"

She should have asked all these questions before. She should have thought to *learn* about the enemy of the temple guardians, her enemies now. She should have asked more questions about the beings whose war could end all the realms.

Erica knew the basic story. But the details... Some of those were lost to time anyway, according to Jilly. But not all. The fact that the Elder-sworn were changeable was known to the others. Erica should have known it too.

"Easily? Yes," Galahad said. "Quickly… Depends on the forms they take."

"Are there limits? Or can they expand to be the size of the wyrm?"

Galahad didn't immediately answer.

This was not a good answer. "Galahad?"

"They can literally be almost anything. Viruses or single celled creatures are beyond them. Their smallest sizes are limited to the macroscopic world. Their largest creatures are also limited."

"But that limit is larger than the wyrm," Morgaine finished, her tone grim.

"Does this mean that instead of the wyrm being able to help us, we have to defend the wyrm as well as retrieve the book to keep it from the Elders?"

"Yes," Morgaine said bluntly. She moved to the side of the spike that allowed her to draw her sword and communicate with those flashes of light to the spike farther along the spine, where Jilly and Memnon were.

Erica moved out of the way, Nimue at her back. The younger cat was keeping herself between Erica and the wall, even when they had to squish backward. Erica wasn't sure if that was reassuring or if she wanted to pull Nimue around so she wasn't in harm's way.

The trick with having a clowder of cats who were supposed to be protecting her? Erica often found herself wanting to keep her cats safe and away from the dangers.

She was going to have to change that soon. The cats were the fighters and guardians. Erica was… not.

Galahad stepped up close to her, so that she was bracketed in by both her cats, and his gaze went to the Elder-sworn keeping pace on the right.

"What's the plan?" Erica murmured to him.

"Morgaine is checking with Jilly and Memnon now. Going back to the surface is an option. Confronting them on solid ground, without the wyrm in the literal middle of things."

"We've been diving for a while. Going back up will also take time. What if they attack before that? What if they attack while we're all like this anyway?"

"We'd be stuck and unable to do much to help the wrym," Galahad said.

"What if the Elder-sworn try to break off the spikes with us in them?" Erica asked her deepest terror out loud. That felt like tempting fate, but also, she needed the answer because there was no point hiding from any of these answers, that wouldn't help her. And hiding from them *now* would be dangerous.

"The spikes aren't that easy to break off," Galahad said. "We will be as safe here during an attack as anywhere. The problem is not being able to help." His hand flexed on the hilt of the sword he'd put back into its scabbard.

Erica could feel the frustration pumping off him. The need to do something about the threat, not just wait inside this narrow spike to see what happened. She didn't know what to say to his frustration, though. She was scared, and afraid anything she'd say would be ridiculous.

She wished she could talk to Jilly, the way the others seemed to be doing with light from their swords. That wasn't something she'd learned to do with her own yet. One day, she'd inherit Alendrial. But not until Jilly stopped being the temple guardian, and Erica was hoping that was a long long way off. Until then, she had her own very good, but not sentient, sword which she'd been training with, learning how to use. But she was still not entirely confident with the basics she'd learned. Swinging a sword around was far from ingrained muscle-memory yet. And she was afraid she'd fail in a fight when she panicked.

So far, that hadn't been an issue. But she was starting to think that was more luck than anything else. And outside of learning how to swing the sword around without cutting herself, she hadn't learned much more.

Glancing at Morgaine, she considered getting her to ask Jilly some questions for Erica. Though she suspected Morgaine was already asking the pertinent ones, like "What do we do now?" and "How do we get out of this without getting killed or getting the wyrm killed?"

The light from Jilly's signal flickered through the darkness, a bright blue series of what Erica thought might be Morse code with longer flickers and short bursts of light. She'd learned Morse code as an undergrad. It had been a very long time, but maybe she could decipher what Jilly was saying at least.

She glanced back to Morgaine, and beyond her to one of the two Elder-sworn keeping pace.

Only to see it flinch and flow farther away from the wyrm.

"Did you see that?" Erica asked aloud.

"What?" Galahad closed the distance between them, though it wasn't much.

She nodded to the Elder-sworn. "It just... I'm not sure how to describe it. It's shape sort of shivered and folded on one side and then it moved farther away." She looked at the other Elder-sworn on the opposite side. It was definitely swimming a lot closer to the wyrm than its companion.

But even as she thought that, one of the strange shivers moved through it and it also swam farther away.

"What the hell?" she murmured. Then a little louder, "Does the wyrm have some sort of self-defense thing he's using? A sonic weapon maybe?" She thought she remembered something about those being good weapons in deep water. Given the way the wyrm communicated, it made sense.

"If he does," Galahad said, "he's never mentioned it before. But I'm not surprised about that."

Neither was she. With only twelve members of his species, it made sense he had some sort of weaponry. He was a freaking dragon after all. Granted one with baleen. But also with teeth, the purpose of which she still didn't know. And he was lined with metallic looking scales and spikes along his back. Some of that had to be for defense against threats, right? Even if the planet hadn't appeared to have anything big enough to threaten a wyrm.

Before the Elder-sworn had shown up.

But they didn't seem to be expanding their size to match the wrym's. And now they were holding a distance. Far enough, she felt less like they might ram the spikes at any moment.

Though, maybe they were just putting in some distance to get their ramming speed up.

She gazed back toward Jilly and Morgaine's light show conversation. Morgaine hadn't stopped even when Erica and Galahad started talking. More light flickered from Jilly's spike.

And the Elder-sworn flinched and moved away again.

That was interesting.

"What's Jilly saying in her messages?" Erica asked Morgaine.

"We're trying to work out how to communicate with the wyrm."

"Does the wrym have any weapons, like sonic weapons it could use against the Elder-sworn?"

"Not that I know of." Morgaine glanced back at her after Jilly's last flickers of light stopped. "Why?"

"The Elder-sworn are…reacting to something. I'm not sure what. But it's like they're getting hit with something and moving farther away every time they get hit."

Morgaine frowned and glanced at the bracketing beings. "That's weird."

"Maybe the wyrm is hitting them with, like, a weird wave or something?" Without being able to ask the dragon, that was going to be really hard to determine.

When a few moments passed, with Morgaine staring at the Elder-sworn instead of responding to Jilly's last message, Erica caught another message from the corner of her eye coming from Jilly's spike.

And because she was watching the Elder-sworn, she saw one flinch again.

"Did you see that?" she asked, a little breathless.

"It flinched," Galahad said.

"Yes, but it flinched when Jilly signaled us."

Morgaine frowned at her, then looked back in the direction of Jilly's spike. "It did?"

"Tell Jilly to send a message again. Anything." Erica moved closer to the spike wall, so she could watch the Elder-sworn better.

"They weren't doing that when I was signaling with Jilly," Galahad murmured. "Were they?"

"I didn't notice it. Nimue?"

"Me neither, and I was watching. Just the last few messages seem to be affecting them." Erica felt Nimue's gaze on the side of her face. "Could it have been something the wyrm was doing just coincidentally at the same time as Jilly's signal?"

Erica's knee-jerk reaction was to say that was some coincidence and probably unlikely. Except she remembered that the wyrm and Jilly had "talked" through Alendrial earlier. Using sound waves.

Could… Could the sword translate the light messages to sound waves for the dragon to hear?

When she asked that out loud, the three cats got very quiet.

"If she can," Morgaine said after a moment, "that would be a new skill she's never demonstrated before."

"But it's not outside the realm of possibility," Galahad finished. "There's a lot about Alendrial we don't know."

Okay. That was fascinating. And when they got back to the temple—she ignored the automatic "if" in that thought—she wanted to discuss this more.

For now, though, "Ask Jilly. It's either the light from Jilly's message. Or the wyrm. And if it's the wyrm, he seems to be hitting the Elder-sworn with…whatever he's hitting them with at the same time as Jilly is messaging with Morgaine. So we need to figure out what exactly is happening."

Because whether it was the light from Jilly's sword or the dragon itself causing the Elder-sworn to flinch, it looked like they had a weapon to fight the creatures now.

They just had to figure out how to use it.

<h1 align="center">Chapter Six</h1>

Erica moved up next to Morgaine, which shifted Galahad and Nimue to the rear of the wyrm spike. "You two keep on eye on the Elder-sworn," she said, her attention on the dark water in front of them where Jilly was. "Say aloud if they react or do anything at all."

Galahad grunted. Nimue agreed with an actual word.

To Morgaine, Erica said, "Can you tell me what Jilly just said."

"She asked what the delay was?" Morgaine's frown creased her dark brow. "Wait, no, she said, 'Why have the Elder-sworn moved? Are you okay?' That was the last message."

"Tell her to signal 'Elder-sworn' with Alendrial

again. Also ask her to signal whatever signifier she uses to reference the wyrm." Jilly hadn't used a name for the wyrm, just Great One and that had made the wyrm laugh, so Erica assumed the honorific wasn't something the wyrm demanded or went by.

Morgaine raised her sword and caught some of the lights from the spike, moving that light along her sword, most of her focus on the weapon's shiny metal as she flicked out her Morse code message. Erica watched the other spike.

Nothing happened when Morgaine signaled to Jilly. The wyrm didn't move. The Elder-sworn didn't move—at least not that Galahad or Nimue mentioned. Everything remained the same.

So it wasn't just any light that caused the Elder-sworn's reaction. And it still might not be the light at all. It could well be the wyrm. Or maybe it was Alendrial? Or maybe it was Alendrial signaling the wyrm to do something?

Too many possibilities. They couldn't fight the Elder-sworn with luck and guess work.

She watched the dark water in front of them, waiting for that blue light signal. When it came, she held her breath.

"She's signaled the words and just the words," Morgaine whispered.

Why she was whispering, Erica wasn't sure, but

probably the same reason Erica was holding her breath.

"They moved again," Nimue said, excitedly. "They did that flinch thing. They were starting to ease closer, but I only realized they'd gotten so close when the moved away again."

"Galahad?" Erica asked without looking away from the place where her aunt was.

"Same on this side."

"Morgaine, have her do it again. Galahad and Nimue. I'm going to raise my hand and drop it the instant the lights from Jilly's spike flash. Tell me how long after that it takes the Elder-sworn to react."

If it was instantly, then it was likely the signal from Alendrial. If it took a few seconds, then either it was the wyrm, or it just took time for the light signal to affect the Elder-sworn. But they were closer. It was definitely something to do with Alendrial and her signaling.

When Jilly's second flickers of light flashed in the dark water, Erica dropped her hand. Then started a count in her head. Two. Three. Four. Five…

"There," Galahad said. "They flinched again. The one on my side is moving farther away." He frowned. "I think they might suspect they've been found out now, though."

"Why?"

"The one on my side is starting to change shape."

"Shit." Erica hurried the two steps to Galahad to look. "Nimue?"

"Mine flinched and moved but isn't—" She cut herself off, then cursed. "Make that is changing too."

"Morgaine, tell Jilly. Tell her they're changing, they've figured out we know something. And to have Alendrial tell the wyrm. Whatever's been hitting them and making them move away, it's likely coming from the wyrm."

She hoped Jilly had already figured all this out. After all, she'd been the temple guardian for years. And she knew how to communicate with the wyrm under non-life-threatening circumstances. But given they had to communicate by light flashes, it was impossible for Erica to judge.

Sure enough, though, even before Morgaine started to message her, Erica spotted lights coming from Jilly's spike. "What's she saying?" she asked Morgain frantically, gripping her arm as the anxiety of what was happening grabbed at her.

Morgaine's head moved as if she were reading long sentences. "She seems to be... She's not signaling us anymore. This is a message to... To the Elder-sworn. I think. She's saying... She's telling the wyrm of the threat—that the Elder-sworn are responding. And then she's also, telling the Elder-sworn to…to essentially fuck off." Morgaine's lip twitched at that.

Erica also found herself wanting to bark out a laugh, but was pretty sure that was more nerves than humor talking.

"They're getting bigger," Galahad warned.

"What do we do from in here?" Erica asked aloud. Panic was starting to creep in. They were, essentially, sitting ducks. The messages had the wyrm reacting earlier but since the Elder-sworn started to change, had the wyrm done anything?

The darkness around them was complete. If not for the bioluminescent creatures floating and bobbing through the blackness, Erica wouldn't be able to see anything at all. She realized the Elder-sworn could really ratchet up the terror by turning off their bioluminescence with their transformation, and suddenly she had a new horror to worry about.

Glancing away from the frantic series of light flickers and streaks coming from Alendrial, Erica studied the Elder-sworn. They were still lit up, but they were definitely bigger now. The flat shape had bulked up too, so it was rounder now, taking on the form of a tube almost.

"Are they taking on the shape of the wyrm?" she asked, her voice choked.

"Possibly," Galahad said. He looked grim, as grim as Erica was panicked.

"Two wyrm-sized beings against one wyrm sounds like bad odds."

"It will be," Galahad said.

Then, so suddenly she even felt the rumble through her feet, the wyrm changed directions. No slow change, no long roll to a different side. The wyrm spun in a circle that sent the four of them flying into the wall without warning.

Erica screamed because she couldn't help it. Galahad grunted as she felt against him and then his arms came up around her, holding her to his chest. Nimue hissed and Morgaine cursed.

And then the harness-like bars that had held them in place as the spikes reattached to the wyrm sealed around their upper bodies again, locking them against the wall they'd just fallen into. The harness was as translucent as the walls still were this time, though, unlike earlier when the harness had looked like the metallic-pearlescent, opaque wall.

All four of them were on one side of the spike, this time, though, much more compacted than the first time. So the harness of wall material wrapped around all four of them together, locking them against the wall and each other.

Erica was locked face-to-shoulder against Galahad's chest, his arms around her back, hers folded between them. She could feel Nimue's shoulder on one side, and Morgaine's back pressed against her other side. Jilly's cat had fallen sideways and seemed at an awkward angle inside the harness, with one shoulder pressed against the wall instead of her back.

"You okay? Everyone okay?" Erica asked. Then clamped her lips shut as the wyrm spiraled so fast it left her dizzy.

When the force of their spin evened enough for them to talk, Morgaine said, "Fine. Not the best position but it'll do. I didn't cut myself with my own sword. That's a bonus."

Erica might have snort-laughed if she wasn't so scared. "Nimue?"

The younger cat hissed again. Then said, "Fine. This is less fun than the last time."

"You said you wanted a rollercoaster."

The wyrm spiraled again, changing directions so that Erica was no longer sure which direction was up or down. The floating lights beyond Galahad's shoulder, all those bioluminescent creatures still visible through the transparent wall, were no help at all because they floated all over the place, no directionality. She hadn't even noticed that before. Very unhelpful.

That she could still see a little, thanks to the blue glow from the walls, and the myriad creatures floating around them, helped mitigate the fear, but only just. Having Galahad's warm, strong body wrapped around her helped too.

She chose not to think too close about that.

The wyrm changed directions again. So fast, Erica thought for sure they'd have been killed by all the tossing around inside the spike if not for the harness. She tried to see what was happening. But the changing positions made everything outside blur and whirl, and her head spun, and she was a little afraid, again, that she might throw up.

Seasickness was nothing to this.

She spotted a long, thin green and yellow trail of light. Another fast change from the wyrm. And then that green and yellow streak of light sailed right past them, over the top of their spike.

She looked up in time to see their spike actually slice through the light.

"Wait, did the wyrm just cut the Elder-sworn?" Her voice choked out as the wyrm spun again and she had to swallow a gasp.

Galahad tilted his head back. "The wyrm is fighting two Elder-sworn. He'll use whatever weapons he has."

"Including the spike we're using for, like, air?" She stared upward and really really hoped the transparent walls were as strong as they'd seemed to be.

A sound like a screech that shivered the walls and was mostly a weird vibration in her ears. Elder-sworn or wyrm? Another of those sounds, this one like a ping, and so high pitched she barely heard it. But it vibrated along her skin.

"I'm feeling the sound," she muttered. "That's weird."

"That's the weird part, huh?" Morgaine asked.

"It's all weird."

Erica gasped again as the wyrm spiraled. Her ears didn't pop, but she could still feel the changing position in a sort of pressure on her skull and in her bones. Or maybe she was imagining that pressure change. She had no idea if they were deeper or higher in the ocean now. The wrym could be heading back to the surface.

She followed another movement of light outside the spike, more green and yellow. Whatever the Elder-sworn had become they were huge now. And between their size, and the wyrm's rapid movements, she couldn't get a good enough look at them to even see what they'd become.

Maybe that was better. Because the sheer size of their lights now was horrifying.

Another rapid spin left Erica's stomach in her throat. She squeezed against Galahad almost unconsciously, glad for both his solid frame and the thick bands of the harness wrapped around her entire upper body.

Especially when her feet lifted off the floor.

"We're diving," Morgaine said.

How she knew, Erica couldn't say, but the minute she'd pointed it out, Erica felt the tilt and movement "downward" or at least moving fast in one direct. She still couldn't tell up from down. Her feet weren't touching the transparent floor anymore, though.

The rapid change in direction left her so disoriented, she wasn't even sure which direction to look for her aunt's spike.

"Is Jilly still signaling with Alendrial?" she asked.

"Not that I've seen," Galahad said, "but it's hard to tell when we're whipping around like this. Morgaine?"

"Too many swirling lights. Can't tell either."

Morgaine was right about all the swirling lights. Because of the speed the wyrm was moving, a lot of the surrounding creatures looked like streaks of color now, smeared out against the black water.

How much deeper were they going? Where were the Elder-sworn? Was the wyrm running away or leading the Elder-sworn into some kind of trap? So many questions and no way to answer them. She just had to hold on for dear life.

The swirling descent seemed to last ages and also happened so fast, Erica was certain they should have all gotten some sort of pressure disease by now. Or maybe that was a fast ascent? She'd snorkeled but never dove, so she couldn't remember. All she knew was that a change in pressure this severe, this fast, should have *felt* like something, shouldn't it?

But outside of the rapid movements with the potential to throw them around inside the spike, she wasn't feeling the pressure of the water around them. Not even ears popping like in an airplane or going through a tunnel.

The knowledge that they were heading downward this fast, though, left her more scared than she wanted to admit out loud. And having Galahad's arms wrapped around her was so comforting, she'd be embarrassed about it later.

If they survived.

CHAPTER SEVEN

The wyrm swirled around and changed directions again, slowing enough that the blurs of light from the bioluminescent beings in the ocean returned to looking like individual creatures. Erica could feel her pulse hammering in her ears, and the terror of where they were and what was following them tightened all the muscles in her stomach.

She'd been scared before, during her training. She had not gotten any more used to it.

The minutes passed with the wyrm gliding along with no additional sharp movements. She looked around, searching the dark waters for the Elder-sworn. Couldn't see them anywhere.

The creatures surrounding them now had changed, though. Many more of them were flatter, some stretched out like flatworms. There also seemed to be more tube-shaped beings. And the colors were much more yellows and oranges than the myriad of rainbow colors earlier.

With all the yellow, she worried finding the green and yellow of the Elder-sworn would be trickier. But then they could change shape, and had, so it made sense they could change their colors too. And might because it was really their colors that had given them away last time.

There were no green-lit creatures that Erica could see anywhere around them. And only a few with the blue illumination. But everything around them was now larger than any of the previous beings.

In fact, everything around them was a *lot* larger now.

"Where are we?" she murmured.

"At the bottom of the ocean now," Galahad murmured.

"And near our destination, I think," Morgaine said.

"The cavern? We're close to it?" Erica's heartbeat didn't stop pounding hard, but now there was an edge of anticipation. She might be terrified by riding in a dragon's spine spike and being chased through black waters by enemies, but retrieving an ancient tomb was the good stuff. That was the reason she'd accepted this destiny.

"We're close," Galahad said.

Now that they weren't tumbling around, her stomach in her throat and the fear of death so close, she became acutely aware of Galahad. His arms around her, the press of her body against his, tight because the wall harness was still firmly wrapped around all of them, keeping them snug against the wall. She was aware of where her arms were folded against his chest. The way his breath fluttered over her temple when he spoke. The musky scent of him.

She winced at that because she realized she smelled like stress sweat. And he had a better sense of smell than she did.

That put a damper on the building…complicated feelings. Which was probably for the best.

But still, having him wrapped around her this way left her very *aware* of him. In a way that was making her face warm. It was good it was so dark and their only light was blue shaded. She was pretty sure that hid her blush.

"What happened to the Elder-sworn?" Nimue asked quietly.

Erica wasn't sure why they were all speaking quietly, nearly whispering, but it felt appropriate for some reason. Maybe it was the utter darkness beyond the walls, punctuated only by the illuminated creatures, not even a hint of the purple shade of the water here. Or maybe it was the fact that they were approaching a sacred place, the place where a mystical and dangerous book had been hidden for eons.

Whatever it was, Erica was glad they were all doing it so she didn't feel ridiculous.

She noticed, though, that no one answered Nimue's question.

The waters around them started to swirl against the spike walls, though it was only obvious in the way the creatures beyond the wall blurred and seemed to stretch and shorten. Something was happening. But without an answer to the Elder-sworn question, she was afraid to ask what was going on.

They passed through a section of water that was so incredibly dark not even other creatures lit up the surroundings. The water seemed to slap more against the clear wall at Galahad's back, where Erica was watching their surroundings, but she couldn't see the movement, just heard a sort of churning sound that was, again, more vibration in her bones than a sound she heard with her ears.

She thought she saw a line of blue flickering lights below where they stood, so she tried to look over Galahad's shoulder and down farther, but her angle was bad for that. The blue light seemed to be coming from the luminescent blue lines under the wyrm's fins, though. It was the only light around them.

Galahad looked over his own shoulder and down. "We're passing through a tunnel," he said. Or rather whispered. "Ancient lava tube."

"Lava? Are we…" She swallowed. "Are we going to encounter lava?" After everything else, running directly into a lava flow this deep under the ocean seemed like a bad idea. Could the wyrm survive a direct hit by lava? That seemed unlikely, but then again, it was an ancient creature that lived in these oceans, so maybe?

"No active lava flows on this part of the planet," Galahad said. "Not anymore. These tunnels are older than the wyrm. Which is very old."

Erica suspected that was an understatement.

"We're almost to the cavern," Morgaine said.

Even as Morgaine murmured that, more lights started to pop on around them. Little glowing white-yellow dots of light. They looked so much like pinpoint stars, Erica breathed out a sigh. They were suddenly surrounded by all those pinpoints of light. And for an instant, it was like they'd launched into space and were traveling through the aether on a dragon's back, riding through the deep space between planets with only the scattered stars to guide them.

The fanciful impression changed abruptly when they swam close enough to a cluster of the lights for her to realize they were small creatures inside the cavern walls. Very small though. She couldn't really see what the creatures looked like. But there were so many of them, they made her think of polyps inside a living coral colony. Just a little bigger.

A sound caught her attention. Or maybe it was the way the translucent floor underfoot started to vibrate. She looked down. Only darkness. Then she looked up.

The cats all looked up with her.

To see a line of churning water working down the outside of the spike.

"We're coming out of the water," Morgaine said.

Galahad's arms tightened around Erica as he whispered, "We're here."

Unable to look away, Erica watched that line of water as it flowed down the spike. As it passed them, the water moving lower, Erica got her first view of the cavern.

And gasped.

It was beautiful. All those little creatures in the walls were still imbedded in the walls, lighting up the darkness so that even though they were literally at the bottom of the ocean, she could still see relatively well. The cavern was a huge space of black rock, smoothed walls that looked almost like glass except for the dots of lit-up polyps. Those walls curved overhead, but she had trouble judging how high overhead, only that the dots of light seemed farther away and there seemed to be room above the tip of the spike so far above her.

There were clusters of different colored lights hanging like stalactites from the ceiling, which also cast white light around the place and lit the surface of the black waters slushing below their feet along the spike walls.

When she looked forward, she could see the other spike now, though only as a faint blue outline. She couldn't see the others inside well. If she stared, she thought she might see larger shadows against one side of the translucent walls, which might well be the others harnessed into place the way she and the cats in her spike were.

"Why are we still all harnessed in?" They weren't swirling or diving or changing directions rapidly anymore. In fact, since they reached the bottom, they'd been gliding so smoothly she barely noticed the movement. Probably wouldn't have noticed they were moving at all if things outside weren't flowing past.

No one answered her question, though, which meant no one else knew for sure.

Or they were afraid to say it out loud.

"Is it because the Elder-sworn are still out there

somewhere and the wyrm might have to move suddenly?"

"It's more to do with what's about to happen," Galahad said against her temple. "This part is supposed to happen, though. Remember that."

"What—?"

Her question cut off abruptly when she felt, rather than heard, a dropping sensation beneath her feet. And then suddenly their spike shot upward, toward the ceiling of the cavern and those dangling collections of lights.

She clamped her teeth together to keep her scream in so it came out sounding like a choked-off squeal, which was embarrassing, but she couldn't help it. Her stomach dropped with the sudden lurch upward, and those fast approaching collections of hanging lights shot a jolt of fear through her.

Then the angle changed and they were falling again, bottom of the spike arrowing back down toward the water. Or the wyrm. She couldn't see beneath her to know.

The descent slowed, unnaturally, and like when they landed on the wyrm's spine, they landed on something solid with a relatively gentle thunk. Gentler than she'd have imagined given the speed they'd dropped back downward.

She waited a moment, looking around, her heart hammering.

The wall harness released, sending all four of them lurching away from the wall at the sudden absence of support. Galahad caught Erica before she fell, holding her upright and only slowly letting her go when she had her balance.

"You okay?" he asked.

She nodded, a little unnerved by…well, everything going on. Suddenly, she couldn't find her voice.

But she was supposed to be the temple guardian here, which meant she had to get her shit together and stop staring up at Galahad like a ninny. She cleared her throat and took a step away from him.

"Nimue? Good?"

The young cat nodded and stared around the cavern outside the spike, her eyes wide.

"Morgaine?"

Morgaine ignored everyone and hurried to one section of the spike, where a moment later, the wall cracked and opened.

The spike that had been their lifeline and only shelter suddenly cracking open, and the hiss of released of air, sent another shock of adrenaline through Erica. A jolt of fear that water would come rushing in and drown them all, even though she could clearly see they were in an air pocket inside the cavern. But when fresh, cold, salty-scented air rushed into the spike, her adrenaline calmed.

Excitement and anticipation rose to replace it.

She was in an underwater cavern, leagues beneath an entire ocean, on an alien planet, delivered here by an alien dragon, after escaping the sworn minions of Elder gods.

Her life had definitely changed in the last few months.

Morgaine was already out the door, rushing toward Jilly and the others. Erica had barely poked her head out of the spike when Nester rushed up to them. "Are you okay? Is everyone okay?"

"Fine. We're all good. You?"

He grunted. "Some wild ride."

"That was my first rollercoaster ride," Nimue said, following Galahad out of the spike. "I liked it at first."

"And at the end?" Nester asked with a grin.

"Still kind of fun."

Nester's deep, booming laugh echoed off the cavern's high ceiling.

Erica looked up to see the stacks of glowing... bugs or fish or whatever they were gathered together like stalactites shiver in the echoing sound. "Maybe we want to talk a little quieter," she said.

"Don't worry," Nester said, giving her a gentle pat on the shoulder. "They're sturdier than they look."

Jilly hurried up to them then. "You're all good. No injuries?"

"No injuries," Erica said, then looked at Nimue and Galahad for confirmation. "What happened? Do know? What happened to the Elder-sworn?"

"The wyrm outraced them to the tunnels. They couldn't take the pressure. They'll be back, though. Or more likely they'll be waiting for us to surface again. We have to get the book and get out of here."

"Right." Erica looked around. "Where is it? And what happened to the wyrm?" Despite the three distinct spikes sticking out of the hard rocky surface of the shore of the cavern, she didn't see any sign of the wyrm itself, even back in the black water that collected close to the shore.

"The wyrm is guarding our backs, making sure the Elder-sworn don't find a way in here."

"How do you know this?"

"Once we realized the wrym and I could communicate through Alendrial underwater, we were able to exchange more information. I've...I've never done that before. I didn't realize it was possible. The wyrm didn't either until it started to overhear the communication between me and you all." Jilly set her hands on Erica's shoulders. "That was very clever of you to figure out what was happening. I wouldn't have realized the wyrm could hear us if you hadn't got us thinking down that path. Thank you."

"I didn't do anything." Erica felt such an overwhelming sense of inadequacy at her aunt's compliments, she couldn't really take them. "Just noticed the reactions happening."

"When no one else did," Jilly said. "Don't underestimate yourself. Remember, you were destined for this."

Given how scared she'd been since the wyrm first appeared, Erica had truly started to doubt if she was destined for this. Maybe her aunt had it wrong. Because she'd been a bit of a mess for most of this adventure.

"It was a scary situation," Jilly said. "I was scared. It's okay to be scared. You came through when you needed to."

Erica nodded, but didn't have any words so she left it at a nod.

Jilly patted her shoulders, then stepped back. "And now we have a book to retrieve."

At least that part was something Erica felt herself capable of. Books were right in her wheelhouse.

Chapter Eight

"This wasn't the kind of book I was expecting," Erica said, staring at the floating collection of light in front of her that didn't look like a "book" in the traditional sense of the word. Or, really, any sense of the word that she knew.

What the book actually looked like was one of the bioluminescent creatures that had been floating in the sea, except the shape of it kept changing. The light itself was a mix of white and pink and purple. Really pretty. But awfully glowy for a book.

It floated in the air above a pool of black water. The pool was small, easy enough to reach across, surrounded by the smooth black rocks of the cavern. None of the little light bugs outside were imbedded in the walls inside this section. It was its own chamber, neither huge nor small, the ceiling far enough they could all walk upright, even Nestor, but not so high Nester or Galahad couldn't have reached the rock overhead by stretching their arm upward.

The scent of damp, fishy, salty air inside the cavern changed a little in this chamber, too. There was a hint of ozone, a flavor of electricity that tingled on her tongue as well as tickled her nostrils.

She wondered if that was the smell of the "book."

No one had reached for it yet.

Even in the temple, Erica had never encountered anything quite like this. And the temple had books that merely opening them could melt a human brain. She didn't go near those books. They stayed on the high shelves at the top of the pyramid. Where she never went. So she wouldn't melt her brain.

Which reminded her… And really, she should have asked this earlier, but, "Is this the kind of book that will melt our brains if we open it?"

"Yes," Jilly said matter-of-factly.

"Uh…" Best response Erica had.

"Or, really, it won't unless we actually try to read it. It's safe enough to handle. Even opening it wouldn't necessarily hurt anyone. It's the reading part you have to look out for. And if we open it, well. Who can resist reading a book after they open it, right? So it's better if we don't tempt ourselves by opening it."

"Fair," Erica choked out. "Good plan. Good plan." She swallowed. As if this adventure hadn't been scary enough. But this part, the book, the way it swirled with light, was made up of light… This part was pretty amazing too.

As they watched the book, it also seemed to… Well to fade in and out of existence. It grew opaque and solid one moment, solid enough she could reach out and touch it. And if she did, she'd be touching solid, physical light in a way that sort of made her brain blink. Then the next moment, the swirling lights grew translucent and ephemeral. Like this thing really was only light, the kind that she could stick her hand through. Nothing really there that was solid enough to grab.

Every time it came back to a more solid light, the shape changed. So it moved from cube, to sphere, to cone, to a shape she didn't have a name for but was definitely more than three dimensional even if she couldn't see all those dimensions, then to a box shape, then to a complex donut.

And once it moved through the shape of a long, serpentine dragon form. Like the wyrm.

"That's a trip," Erica said, her voice quiet and awed even to her own ears.

"It's a very unique book," Jilly agreed with a nod.

"There are eleven more like it?"

"None of them are quite the same. But… Essentially, yes. Eleven more. Twelve all together. And while each, individually, is valuable because…"

Jilly waved a hand at the "book," and Erica knew exactly what she meant without having to ask. It was valuable because it was what it was and what it was was amazing.

"But combine the twelve together," Jilly said with a headshake and a sigh. "Cataclysmic if they all fall into the wrong hands. That's why they were separated. Why they've remained hidden and separated for most of the age of this Universe."

"This Universe?"

"This realm? Whichever word you prefer. There are many of them."

Jilly always talked about the many different realms. Erica wasn't entirely sure why she never thought of those realms as other *universes*, because of course they were. But then, she was a historian, not a cosmologist or universe scientist. She wasn't even a science historian. Those thoughts went beyond her particular realm of expertise.

Used to anyway. She might have to expand her

knowledge on that front if she was going to keep doing her current destined job.

"Why would anyone…anything create these in the first place if they're so dangerous?" she asked.

Jilly shrugged. "Who knows. Ancient gods and god-like beings doing things because they can, without thinking of consequences? Maybe at the time they were created they were needed, required to do something important or fix something damaged, or just…a repository of knowledge in the way that our temple is. We can't read them. And only have an idea of what they are and what they do because of knowledge passed down in other sources, knowledge kept with the wyrms guarding them. We do know they're dangerous when combined. And that the Elders and the Wraiths will use them in their war. And that would be bad for every living being across all the realms. So we guard them, and hide them, and keep them separated. And have to accept that we'll never know for sure why anyone brought something this dangerous into existence."

Erica hated that. She wanted to *know* things. Wanted explanations for *why* things were done the way they were or how they were done or what was going through the minds of the people who did them. It was that curiosity that had driven her to history in the first place, and her specific field of social history in particular.

Having no answers, no way of confirming or even getting hints to answer the *why* questions was irritating.

"It's either accept that you'll never know or melt your brain," Jilly said. "I would prefer you didn't melt your brain."

"Me to." Erica sighed. "But I'd still love answers to *why*."

"Wouldn't we all," Jilly said.

"How do we get it out of here?" They did have a time crunch. Erica would have to mull over the existential crisis of this book's existence later.

The pool over which the book floated wasn't so wide they couldn't easily reach over it and grabbed the book. But no one had made a move to reach for it yet. And the seconds were ticking past. A slight dripping sound from just outside the chamber even set the timing, like a metronome. *Drip, drip, drip* went the seconds as they just stood there staring at the potentially brain-melting, light-changing tome.

"We're waiting for it to come into a specific shape. If we grab for it in some of the other shapes…" Jilly paused. Then, "Well, let's just say, that would be bad."

"Right. Worse than brain-melting bad?"

"Depends on how much you like your connection to the temporal plane."

"Quite a bit actually."

"As I thought. So we wait for the correct shape."

"Okay." Erica watched the swirling white and pink and purple lights move through another series of shapes, some of which she couldn't really comprehend. Then, "What shape are we waiting for?"

"A very precise box shape. It will look like a large portfolio book, something with dimensions that feel *right* for a human brain and yet still larger than, say a hardback in a bookstore."

Erica found her head nodding as if she understood exactly what Jilly meant even though she was having a hard time understanding what Jilly meant.

Then suddenly, the book's light solidified into the exact shape Jilly had just described. It was *the* shape, though Erica wasn't entirely sure how she knew it was the right shape. The book had flowed through similar configurations before this. But this time... She was certain this was the one.

And without even thinking about it, she reached over the small pool and grabbed the book before it could change again or fade until it was nothing but light.

She blinked at the feel of it as she pulled it toward her. It felt solid in her hand. But it didn't precisely *look* solid in her hand. The lights swirled around her fingers and palm, and the scent of ozone got stronger. But holding the book didn't hurt. There weren't any tingles or heat or coldness. If she closed her eyes, she'd just feel a solid, coffee table sized hardback book in her hand, with a cover that had a smooth texture, and a slightly awkward shape she had to hold carefully.

"Wow," she murmured.

Jilly exchanged a look with Memnon, who'd been standing at her side. Then looked back at Erica. "You... You didn't hesitate to take up the book."

"You said we needed this shape. That it was the only shape, right? I didn't want it to fade back out. No telling how long we'd have to wait for the specific shape again." Since they hadn't seen it before that moment after watching the book for several minutes.

"But it's been in similar shapes before. You knew *this* one was the right one."

"Weird. I know. But I did. It was obvious at the time." She frowned at her aunt, at Memnon. "Was I not supposed to know?"

"On the contrary," Jilly said. "The fact that you did know so instinctively, and that you didn't hesitate to touch the book, is very good. As temple guardian you're *supposed* to know these things, even if only on instinct rather than actual experience."

"Did you? Know I mean. When you first saw the book?"

Another look exchanged with Memnon. "I... I knew. But I didn't touch the book."

"Was I not supposed to?" Erica held the swirling light book in front of her, looking at it in fear. Except... She could feel it, it wasn't hurting her, this was the shape Jilly said they needed to touch the thing, and they were here to get it out. So they had to pick it up.

"You were supposed to," Jilly said. "I just... didn't think you would. Yet. But this is good. This is fine."

"Been hearing the word 'fine' a lot today and then getting chased by Elder-sworn while riding the back of a dragon inside one of said dragon's spine spikes, so I'm starting to question your understanding of that word."

Jilly snort-laughed and shook her head. "Let's get out of here. We still have Elder-sworn to get past." She gestured to the book. "You get to keep that with you. Now that you've touched it, it's bound to you until we get it to the temple. You're its new, official guardian."

"Oh shit." That's why they'd done the look exchange, wasn't it? She'd accidentally linked herself to the book. "I'm its new wyrm now, aren't I?"

"I'm afraid so. But it was inevitable. One of us had to take the wyrm's job. That's why we're here."

"A heads up would have been nice." Erica gave her aunt a level look.

"You were having enough trouble adapting to the wyrm's existence. I thought I'd have time to explain. Too late now. We need to leave."

The cats formed up around her and Jilly as they left the chamber and walked out into the wider cavern, toward the shore where the ocean waters looked like a calm lake, tiny waves of movement lapping the smooth black rocks.

The book's lights outshone the little light bugs imbedded in the walls and the clusters of lightbugs hanging from the ceiling far overhead. The purple and white glow from the book brightened the cavern so much, it almost looked like daylight, stretching their shadows behind them.

"What happens if I put the book down?" Erica asked.

"Just... Don't." Jilly stopped to look her dead in the eyes. "You will need to hold tight to that until we step back into the temple. It won't hurt you. You can wrap your arms around it, move it from hand to hand, anything necessary. But you can't put it down. You have to hold it now."

"I really should have known about this fine print earlier," Erica said.

"Yes. Live and learn."

"Live and—" Erica's squeak of outrage was cut off by the wyrm rising out of the smooth surface of the water.

"Time to go," Jilly said, her voice all business now. "Back into your assigned spikes, everyone. Now."

Erica still intended on having words with Jilly. But her aunt was right about one thing. They had to get out of here.

They had to reach the surface and the way back to the temple.

Before the Elder-sworn reached them.

Chapter Nine

Erica rode inside the spike harnessed against the wall, all the way back to the surface. She was terrified of dropping the book after Jilly's dire, if vague, warning, and she didn't want to risk dropping it with a sudden change of direction if they had to fend off the Elder-sworn again.

When, she thought grimly. When they had to fend off the Elder-sworn again.

Jilly must have communicated the need to keep Erica harnessed in with the wyrm, or else the wyrm just realized this was important—and why wouldn't he since *he* probably already knew that once the book was picked up, the holder couldn't put it down. At any rate, Erica didn't have to do anything or ask the wyrm to keep her harnessed in—not that she knew how—because the wyrm just kept the harness on her all the way to the surface.

How they made it back to the surface without trouble, she wasn't sure, but she was glad for the relatively swift, uneventful ride.

"How are we not getting the bends or something?" she asked Galahad when she realized they were climbing fast. The bioluminescent beings outside the translucent spike wall blurred past on the way through the black water.

Galahad had stayed beside her, freed from his own harness but still never moving away from her side, for the entire trip. The other two cats had taken up positions at different points opposite her, staring out the wall at the passing creatures and ocean, on the lookout for the Elder-sworn's return.

"The spikes are pressurized," Galahad said. "Like being inside an airplane. No gas bubbles building in our blood under higher pressure."

"Ah. Cool. Didn't know that." She was nervous and looking for something to think about other than dropping the light book.

For its part, the Book of Time stayed a solid thing in her arms, felt solid enough anyway. And though the harness covered over her arms, to keep her in place and, she suspected, to keep the book in her arms—because the wyrm was clever and old and had dealt with humans before and probably knew a startle reflex was entirely too possible—the book's swirling show of pinks and purples and white made it look a bit like her upper body was wrapped in a blanket made of light. The glow from the book seemed to brighten the interior of their spike more than the wyrm's natural blue glow. She'd worried about that at first, standing out to the other beings in the water. To the Elder-sworn.

But the Elder-sworn already knew they were riding the dragon's back. And the other creatures didn't seem inclined to mess with a dragon at any rate.

She tried to avoid looking down at the book. When she did, it made her head swim because her brain had trouble comprehending the difference between what she could see and what she could feel. What she felt was the solid portfolio-sized book object in her arms. What she saw was swirling lights and her hands moving in and out of solidity with the object shifting through shapes and…existence.

Once, and only once, she'd looked down to see the book not really there anymore. Some of the light, but mostly her eyes saw her hands gripping empty air. Her instinct, her near reaction, had been to open her hands wide and look for the thing that should have been there but wasn't anymore.

That would have resulted in her dropping the book she could clearly still *feel* in her grip.

Which, according to Jilly, would have been bad.

So Erica had stopped looking at the book all together, letting the fact that she felt it in her arms be enough to reassure her she still held it. The lights still reflected up around her. Occasionally, she caught a larger swirl of light below the edge of her focus. But she resolutely refused to look.

And was extremely grateful for the wyrm's harness wrapping around her arms and entire upper body.

When they finally broke the ocean surface, at first Erica wasn't sure they were really there. The white churning waves around them glowed a little like the creatures in the ocean, and while the waves slapped against the spike up to a certain level but above that level there was no movement and no more of the glowing undersea critters, it was still so dark she felt like they must still be underwater.

She looked up and saw the stars spreading out overhead. Constellations she'd never seen before. Thick in all directions instead of just that strip of thick stars that marked the edge of the Milky Way. And just rising high enough to see over the rolling ocean waves, a bright orange moon, smaller than Earth's moon, but perfectly round. Above it, and farther away, Erica was pretty sure that large dot of light was also a moon.

The movement of the wyrm swimming on the

surface rocked her in a way she hadn't felt below the surface, so she went back to worrying about dropping the book even though the harness was still firmly wrapped around her.

"Almost there," Galahad said quietly.

"Then what? And where are the Elder-sworn?"

"Then, we return to the temple and get that book stored safely."

"In the highest rafters so no one's brain melts."

"Something like that." His lips twitched, but he didn't quite smile.

Really, it wasn't a smiling moment but she felt like she'd missed a rare opportunity to see his smile.

"As for the Elder-sworn…" He frowned at the waves beyond the spike's still translucent wall. "I'm not sure where they are."

"That's bad, right? Worse that we don't know where they are."

"It's…not good."

She couldn't see the shore approaching, but if she stretched her head back against the spike wall and looked *just* right, she could see the cliffs in the distance. "Why are the spikes still see-through? I figured they'd go opaque again at the surface."

"I don't know. Maybe because it's nighttime? They went opaque the last time we were here, but also we resurfaced in the middle of this planet's daytime. That's the only real difference."

"That and the Elder-sworn."

Galahad's mouth flattened, his expression grim.

"Is there a plan?" she asked. She hadn't heard one, but that didn't mean the cats and Jilly didn't have a sort of standing procedure for situations like this that they just hadn't gotten around to telling Erica yet. She didn't *think* they kept secrets from her on purpose, but she was starting to realize they had a shorthand among them and sometimes actually forgot to fill her in on the details behind that shorthand.

She supposed, after years of working together, she and her own cats would reach that stage. That seemed a long way off now.

Morgaine finally turned away from her vigilant sentry duty to say, "We'll reach the beach soon."

Then she waited. As if she expected someone else to expand on the plan for when that beach-reaching happened.

All three cats looked at Erica.

She stared back. It took a moment before she realized they were waiting for her to say something.

To give them the plan of action.

When she'd been waiting for one of them to give her the plan of action.

Ah. Shit. She didn't know what to do. She was too new to this and still in training and there was so much she didn't know. She wasn't the leader yet.

That was Jilly. Jilly knew what to do on adventures, and Erica followed along and learned. Sometimes the hard way, but still…

She wasn't the *leader* yet. Not even close.

She swallowed. "Jilly will have a plan, right?"

Morgaine nodded. But then didn't elaborate. She just blinked her big brown eyes at Erica.

Erica blinked back. "Okay. Well. I guess we, uh, follow that plan…?"

Morgaine nodded again, gave a little shrug and looked back out the spike at the dark night and churning ocean.

So. That was it? That was all she'd expected from Erica?

That wasn't too hard. Just pass off all the responsibility to Jilly.

Erica ignored the voice that whispered she wouldn't be able to do that forever. Eventually, she'd be the one in charge. But since that meant Jilly would be dead, Erica hoped that time wasn't for years and years and years yet.

"Jilly's plan will probably involve racing back to the cat tree and returning to the temple as fast as possible," Galahad put in. Spoken casually. Not like he was making a point of telling Erica the plan she obviously didn't known. Just saying what they all knew out loud. Casual like.

She appreciated the effort even if they both

knew better. "Good plan if we can reach the tree before the Elder-sworn attack."

The silence inside their spike as they approached the shore was a solid living thing between them filled with tension and anticipation. Maybe a little dread? Or maybe the dread was just on Erica's part. The cats had been in this fight for a lot longer than her.

A rumbling vibration filled the spike walls, rolling through the soles of Erica's feet. Without a word, the cats all turned their back to the wall of the spike as the harnesses formed and wrapped around them again, the feet clamps rising up over everyone's boots—including Erica's now.

This was it. They were about to get shot out onto the beach. She looked around, frantically looking for some sort of attack, some sign of the Elder-sworn. The lights from the Book of Time flickered beneath her eyeline, calling her to look down and confirm she still held the book. But she ignored the impulse. She could still feel it. Her eyes would just mess with her head if she looked.

Another rumbling beneath her feet. And then they were suddenly, stomach droppingly, shot straight upward into the air.

She felt this launch more than the ones below the ocean. Felt the pull of gravity stronger and harder, the g-forces holding her against the wall as much as the harness. Then the peak, the drop, the surprisingly gentle landing.

Somewhere in the launch and drop, the walls went opaque again. That shimmering pearlescent silver color that reminded her of both pearls and metal.

The opaque walls meant she couldn't see where they landed or if the others had landed. And that made her anxious to get out of the harness and out of the spike. She was practically dancing in place, even though her feet were fixed to the floor by the foot clamps and her upper body was still secured to the wall.

She felt the lure to look down at the book she could clearly still feel in her arms. The harness released, the foot holds retracted, she took her first step from the wall since boarding the spike in the cavern under the ocean. The temptation to look down got worse.

Lights danced below her chin, brighter now, lighting up the entire interior of the spike. She only realized how dark the interior had gotten then. And that the book's swirling pink and purple light was their only illumination.

Before anyone even spoke, the spike cracked open, releasing the stored air and letting a fresh, sharp breeze swirl through the open space. Erica rushed to the opening, in a hurry to check on her aunt. In an even bigger hurry to get back to the temple. The fear of dropping the book kept her muscles tight.

Galahad put a hand on her shoulder before she stepped outside, though. "Let me go first. Just in case." When she opened her mouth to say something—though she wasn't sure what or why she wanted to protest since he was supposed to be her guard—he said, "I have my hands free to fight. You do not. This is our job. Trust us."

"I do." She nodded and stepped back so he and the other two cats would have room to get out first. She did trust them. And he was right. She couldn't exactly fight at that moment, even if she'd been better with the sword strapped to her hip, because it would require loosening her hold on the book and she didn't dare do that.

The three cats eased out of the spike, fanning out on the pink sand beach beyond. Erica watched from the opening, but kept just inside in case she needed to duck back behind cover. Galahad gave a low whistle and she finally stepped outside.

Except for the three spikes, and all the cats fanned out in front of them, the beach was empty.

This didn't stop Erica's heartbeat from hammering. It just meant she didn't know where the threat was coming from yet.

She watched Jilly step out from the spike. She'd

come out last too. Which kind of surprised Erica. Jilly's hands were free to use her sword.

But the cats *were* their bodyguards. They were there to protect Jilly, to protect Erica. And Erica had to get used to letting them do their job.

A lot she still had to get used to.

"Let's get back to the temple," Erica said, impatient to rush to the tree that looked a bit like seaweed and drift wood all at the same time. Their escape route was clear.

"The Elder-sworn can shape-change," Galahad reminded her in a quiet voice.

Oh. Oh shit. She'd forgotten that. The empty beach wasn't necessarily empty.

The Elder-sworn could be…anywhere.

Chapter Ten

The night wind blew across Erica's face as she scanned the open pink sands, looking for an anomaly, anything that would indicate the Elder-sworn were there. From behind the spikes, she heard the ocean surging, the huge waves that never quite made it up onto the shore as anything but a gentle shooshing. She glanced back and around the edge of the spike. The whitecaps were still glowing enough to rival a moon's light, giving the night more illumination than she'd first thought stepping out of the spike.

Something big moved through that light. A shadow cutting up through the huge swells and then dropping beneath the surface again.

"Is that the wyrm or the Elder-sworn?" she

asked, keeping her gaze on the ocean, trusting the cats to watch the other areas of the beach.

"The wyrm," Jilly said, her voice carrying clearly over the sand. "How's the book?"

"Safe so long as I don't look down."

"Then don't look down."

"Helpful." Erica watched that rising and lowering shadow and wasn't sure Jilly was right about it being the wyrm because... "There are no spine spikes," she said. "On the shadow out there in the waves. No spine spikes. I don't think that's the wyrm."

Jilly turned to face the sea. Erica glanced at her long enough to see her scowl. Alendrial glowed in the darkness, a soft blue that lit the area around Jilly. Erica had only seen the sword do that inside the temple.

Erica looked back to the waves, to the shadow rising out of the swells only to disappear again.

The crunch of sand behind her had her spinning to face a new threat... Which turned out to be Galahad. She quickly looked beyond him. The other cats were still guarding their backs. But Memnon and Galahad had moved up next to their respective temple guardians. Memnon stood at Jilly's side, his intent gaze out on the ocean.

Galahad had moved up just behind Erica and his attention was on her.

"We need to get you back to the temple. Now. The others will hold off the Elder-sworn. Once you're through the portal, they'll back off and the others can return."

"That sounds both dangerous and risky. What if the Elder-sworn try to get back to the temple with us?"

"They won't get past the others." He nodded down at the book without looking at it. "Right now, keeping that from the Elders is our most important task. Everything else is irrelevant."

Everything else? Did he mean everyone else's lives? Because she wasn't going to be okay with that, even if they were prepared to lay their lives down to get this done.

"Go," Jilly shouted. "Your cats will have your back. Mine will have mine. That's the way this works."

"Leaving you behind on this beach is not how this works," Erica said, though her gaze was on Galahad.

"It is," Jilly said. "It'll be okay. Get to the portal."

A huge sound of water falling behind her had Erica facing the ocean again. From the waves, rose a dark shadow that was nothing like anything she'd seen as they dove. It was black, and slick, reflecting some of the light from the whitewater on the waves.

There were tentacles and a bulbous body, a bit like a squid, but there also seemed to be a spike tipped tail and a mouth with teeth.

"Elder-sworn?" she asked.

"Elder-sworn," Galahad confirmed.

"Run!" Jilly shouted.

Erica ran. She clung to the book, holding it tight to her chest, and scrambled over the soft sand, aiming for the tree portal. Galahad right beside her. He caught her whenever she stumbled in the sand, holding her upright with one hand on her elbow.

He had his sword in the other.

She glanced back once to see Nester and Nimue taking up the rear behind Galahad. Following fast behind them but pausing every few steps to check their rear.

"Keep going?" Galahad said.

She caught a glimpse of the Elder-sworn surging toward shore and then faced the portal again.

They were within a few feet of it, when another dark shadow rose up from the sand and Erica skidded to a stop.

"Why did you—?" Galahad cut himself off as he saw the shadow, too.

It rose and rose. And rose. Until it was a towering form made of shadow and weird dots of inner light like stars across its surface. It was so close, she couldn't see the shape it had taken. Only that it was huge. And had tentacles like the thing in the ocean.

She opened her mouth to curse, but choked it back when the Elder-sworn swung a tentacle at her and she found her self on the ground with Galahad covering her.

The book felt momentarily insubstantial in her grip and she started to panic. But then the feel of it solidified again. She still didn't dare look at it. It hadn't hit the ground. She'd turned so she lay on her shoulder and back. Galahad was braced over her rather than laying on top of her. The whole thing awkward. But she'd escaped the deadly swing of that tentacle and kept the book from the ground and that was the important part.

Nester roared and charged the shadow. To Erica's surprise, he tore right through the base of it, cutting the shadows to ribbons with his sword. There was no blood but a lot of wispy black smoke that floated off and made the Elder-sworn shriek.

The sound was so loud and piercing, Erica came very close to releasing her hold on the book to cover her ears. She could only imagine how horrible that sound was to the cats. She'd never heard anything quite like it. A shriek, yes, but one so sharp and high and deep and long it felt like a curse.

Felt. Not sounded. The sound was something her brain refused to translate as sound.

"Come on," Galahad lifted her back to her feet, with a strength she'd think about later if they survived, and ushed her toward the portal, trying to skirt the Elder-sworn as Nimue charged past him, joining Nester in the attack.

Nimue was new to this, almost as new as Erica, and so Erica had a soft spot for her. Watching the young cat charge something the size of the Elder-sworn sent a jolt of adrenaline-fueled terror through Erica.

Until she saw the younger cat tear another smoking hole through the creature.

Another of those head splitting noises and the black smoke rushed away on the breeze.

Erica realized the Elder-sworn was a little smaller than it had been a moment before. Or at least it seemed ever so slightly less massive. But that could have been her imagination.

Behind her, near where the ocean met the beach, she heard a roar. A massive amount of water shooshing fast. Some shouts.

She glanced back to see the other Elder-sworn attacking the cats on shore. To see Jilly charging in with Alendrial raised.

Erica was so torn between her own escape and going to help Jilly, she did nothing but stand in place for a dangerous three seconds. Then Galahad got her moving again.

They raced toward the seaweed like portal as Nester and Nimue continued to attack the Elder-sworn on the beach, avoiding its flailing tentacles with surprising dexterity. Why Erica was surprised, she wasn't sure. They were cats after all.

She and Galahad were within steps of the portal when another huge, terrible sound made them both stop in their headlong run to turn back toward the ocean.

The spikes that had been on the beach shot into the air, leaving a cloud of sand behind. They rose high overhead and dropped back fast to the ocean.

Cutting through the Elder-sworn on their way.

"I... I didn't know they could do that," Erica murmured.

"Me neither," Galahad said.

The Elder-sworn made one of those horrifying shrieks as the spikes passed through it, opening up wounds that, on this being, bled a black slick oily substance instead of the smoke spilling from the being on the beach.

From the churning waves behind the bleeding Elder-sworn, another dark shadow rose. This one with rows of blue lights under its fins.

The dragon swung its tail up and through the Elder-sworn, spikes along the ridge of the tail cutting through the squid-like creature like a series of knives. Another shriek as the wyrm disappeared beneath the waves again.

Jilly signaled her cats and they all hurried farther back on the beach, away from the violently churning sea, away from the now flailing Elder-sworn.

A shriek from the creature on the beach and it abandoned its fight with Nester and Nimue to charge the water, flying into the waves on the breeze, moving so fast, it blurred.

Jilly and all the cats hurried toward Erica and Galahad, Jilly and Memnon taking up the rear, watching the two Elder-sworn as they circled each other in the water, causing the ocean to spin up into a water tornado.

"This is bad, isn't it?" Erica asked.

"Could be better," Galahad said.

"Could be worse," Nester said when he reached them.

Nimue waved a frantic hand at Erica. "We have to get you and the book through the portal."

Erica made a move to do just that, but paused yet again when something leapt out of the water and arrowed directly through the Elder-sworn's water tornado. Whatever it was, it blurred, but Erica got the impression of length, and reflective silver light, and bulk. And she was pretty sure she caught spine spikes and blue dots of light.

The Elder-sworn shrieked. And then spikes

pierced up through the creature that bled oil. A blast of light danced over its black body like blue lightning racing around it. The smoke-bleeding Elder-sworn reached for its companion and the blue lightning caught it, covered it.

The lightning was so bright, it lit up the beach more than the red sun had, so bright it was momentarily daylight.

Erica could practically see the interior structure of the two Elder-sworn, though her brain didn't comprehend it so never really resolved what she seeing into a picture she'd remember. The Elder-sworn screamed, both of them, as the lightning tightened around them like rope and squeezed.

The squeeze shrunk them. Forced them to smaller and smaller shapes. Until they were only about the size of the jellyfish-like forms they'd taken when Erica and the others had first spotted them. So small, Erica could barely see them in the churning ocean but for the lightning still sparking around them.

She thought the creatures might just wink out of existence under the pressure of that lightning. But then a huge form rose up above them from the sea. The blue lines of light and waving fins now obvious in the glow from the blue lightning. The wyrm's huge head high above the shrunken Elder-sworn.

The wyrm opened its mouth, and Erica watched

with wide eyes as the baleen folded back and teeth dropped down from the wyrm's jaw. That huge mouth arrowed down toward the ocean.

Clamping around both the Elder-sworn at once.

The wyrm opened its mouth once to chomp better. Erica blinked, though she couldn't really make out what was happening inside that teeth-filled mouth, a fact she was extremely grateful for. And then the wyrm's mouth closed and it dove beneath the ocean again, a long slow roll of its giant form, the spine spikes fanning in a deadly wave as it sank into the water.

She swallowed hard. "Did it just eat the Elder-sworn?"

"Might have," Galahad said.

"Thought you said it didn't eat anything larger than krill."

"It doesn't. For sustenance."

"But for…defense?"

"Defense. Good word for that."

"Thank you for not telling me about what it actually does with its teeth earlier."

"You're welcome."

Jilly hurried up to them. "Why are you still here? Let's go."

"The wyrm just ate the Elder-sworn," Erica said. "Why are we still in a hurry?"

"Because that book will attract more and

because if we don't get it to the temple soon, it'll enter a temporal loop and we won't be able to retrieve it."

Erica blinked. "What? Why didn't you warn me?"

She could still feel the book but the lights below her eyeline were starting to churn more now that she wasn't blinded by wyrm lightning.

"Gotta go," Jilly said.

Erica wanted to demand more answers, but she'd do that once they got back to the temple.

Galahad stood beside the appropriate branch in the seaweed looking collection of branches and motioned her through.

She took one last look at the alien beach, the purple ocean churning under starlight. The whitewater in the waves glowing.

No more Elder-sworn. And no more wyrm.

She turned and stepped into the portal.

<h1 style="text-align:center">CHAPTER ELEVEN</h1>

The minute Erica exited the huge, deep blue cat tree on the other side of the portal and stepped in the temple, she felt her shoulders relax and her muscles ease. She moved away from the tree so the others could get through. And once the last one, Memnon, stepped into the temple, Erica wobbled and abruptly sat down on one of the many pillows scattered across the floor, still clutching the Book of Time to her chest.

The interior of the temple was just one huge open space inside a golden sandstone pyramid, the galleries going up getting progressively smaller. All the really dangerous books were kept at the top of the temple, in places that were hard to reach. That would be where they put the book they'd just retrieved, and she'd be happy to finally be able to let it go.

The ground floor of the temple was all tables and shelves and stacks of books. The stone floors covered with rugs and pillows and chairs. The cat tree portal took up one whole corner of the square base of the pyramid, and when she'd first seen it, she'd been warned she wasn't ready for that portal yet.

Sometimes she still didn't feel ready for it, even though she'd been through it twice now. They used other portals outside the temple for other retrievals, and to get back to hers and Jilly's realm, the portal on this side that led to the cat tree in her apartment was a giant tree in the forest of giant things surrounding the temple. But for some specific places, apparently the only way to get there was by the temple tree.

It was a good thing there were pillows and a chair near the tree.

"You okay?" Galahad asked, crouching down beside her.

"We're all back here and we're all alive. I'm great." She grinned tiredly.

He grinned back, which did a lot for reviving her soul. "The book?"

She glanced down at the swirling light entity in her arms. It was no longer swirling with light.

The book now was just that portfolio-sized book, perfectly solid, no more wavering in and out of existence—or at least appearing to do so if she looked at it—and no more slashes and swirls of pink and purple and white light. The cover was a solid purple leather now, with no marking except for a raised circle of the same colored leather. Just an ordinary circle. Nothing inside it or outside it. Not even a different color. And it wasn't particularly thick either. A narrow spined photo album. That was what it looked like now.

She ran her fingers over the circle. And despite herself, and Jilly's warnings, she did want to open the book, to peak inside. But she knew herself well enough to know if she did that, she would absolutely start trying to read it. Which would melt her mind. Which would defeat the point of surviving the Elder-sworn attack.

Loosening her tight grip on the book, she lifted it and showed it to Jilly, who was standing with Memnon a few feet away. The rest of the cats had scattered throughout the temple, and she spotted some of them in their cat forms again, while others had remained in human form. She was pretty sure Nester was retrieving some of the wine and whiskey they kept here for celebrating jobs well done.

Erica could use some whiskey about now.

"We can put it up now, right? I can let it go and nothing horrible will happen?"

"You can let it go now," Jilly said. "In fact, I'll take that off you, and Memnon can place it where it belongs."

"High up in the rafters," Erica said as she handed the book to Jilly. "High. High up there. At the very tip. Way far away from anyone who might decide to open it."

Jilly didn't laugh at Erica's sudden enthusiasm for great heights. Instead, she stared at the cover of the book for a long long moment, also tracing the circle on the leather with her fingertips.

"This book has remained in wyrm care for longer than the Milky Way has existed," she said quietly. "It's one of the most ancient books here. And we have books from near the beginning of the universe."

"There are *books* from the beginning of the universe? Who the hell would have made them?"

"Books in this realm start..." Jilly shrugged. "Depends on who you ask. Gods. Universal intelligences. Beings from other realms tossing the books in here to get rid of them. At any rate, the Book of Time, all twelve of the books, are books that date back to near that time. So old." She passed her thumb over the circle again. "And even knowing what might happen, I can hardly resist opening this.

Just to see. To really see what the interior looks like."

Memnon, watching Jilly closely, frowning, finally reached out for the book. "Ready to put that away now?" The question was…deliberate.

Erica found herself holding her breath even though she wasn't completely sure why she was or why the tension in their small group was suddenly so high.

Jilly hesitated for a long moment. Then handed the book to Memnon and shook her hands. She gave Erica a small eye roll. "The temptations of some of these tomes is an issue." She narrowed her eyes at Erica. "You were tempted to open it?"

"Sort of. But also very aware of the whole brain melting thing. Do not want. So that made it easier not to open the book."

Jilly made a sort of non-committal noise. Then nodded. "Good. That…explains a lot."

"Explains what, exactly?"

"Why you were the one compelled to grab and hold the book instead of me. Why you saw the shape faster than the rest of us. Why the book chose you to carry it here."

"The book chose me?"

Jilly nodded.

"I need a drink."

Jilly laughed and Erica watched Memnon's shoulders relax.

"I'll put this away. You break open the wine." He headed off into the temple.

Erica had no idea how he got to the upper parts of the temple. She hadn't been shown the way and frankly it was one of the few things she didn't push for answers. Better not to even know how to get to the really scary books.

Especially since the idea of looking at books that had existed from the very beginning of time was so damned tempting.

"You told me once," Erica said to Jilly as Galahad gave her a hand up from the pillow she'd collapsed onto. "You told me once that one day I'd be able to read some of those brain melting books without melting my brain. But that's not true for all of them."

Jilly shrugged. "Not all of them. You will be ready to read from some of them one day, though."

"Don't worry. I'm not in a hurry." Not really anyway. She was curious. Of course she was. But not enough for the risk. And also, she just didn't know how to get to those books.

She still wasn't going to ask.

"Let's get good and drunk," Jilly said. "We've earned it."

Jilly joined Nester in selecting the wine—

Memnon was picky about his wines—and left Erica and Galahad to join everyone else at a slower pace.

The…thing between them still hovered there, complicated and a little unnerving. But when they were here, and they were both relaxed, she thought more about those complicated feelings. Like she was at that moment.

She paused to look up at him, but then wasn't sure what she'd meant to say. Meeting his curious and steady gaze left her breathless. Talk about brain melting.

Finally, she cleared her throat and just said, "Thanks for everything there. As always. Thank you."

"Of course." He blinked and glanced down at the floor before meeting her gaze. "You are doing a good job. In your training. I'm not sure you realize that. But you are doing great. You are going to make an excellent temple guardian."

Her turn to blink. Hard. Because his words hit a sensitive spot she hadn't realized might make her teary-eyed. An insecurity that had plagued her during this retrieval. She swallowed back the emotions, the tears that would make them both uncomfortable and embarrassed, and when she could manage, she said quietly, "Thanks for that, too."

He brushed his fingers over her cheek. A quick,

gentle, barely-there touch that still managed to make her heart thump. She watched him swallow hard and his gaze dropped to her mouth. And none of that helped her breathing or the rapid pace of her heartbeat.

Then he straightened away from her and forced a smile that looked strained at the edges and said, "Ready for a drink?"

"Yes," she said with feeling, forcing her own smile.

They joined the others, and Erica did just as Jilly had suggested and got good and drunk.

She very deliberately didn't think about alien dragons eating shape-shifting Elder-sworn. And even more deliberately didn't think about the complicated feelings that lay between her and Galahad.

Brain melting *books* were more than enough for one day.

Thank You

Thanks for reading this dragon themed edition of the Haunts and Howls collections! I hope you enjoyed the dragon stories in all their varieties. Honestly, I could write many more collections of dragon stories because there are a never-ending variety of dragons tales (and tails? Sorry.) to explore.

If this is your first Haunts and Howls collection, be sure to check out the others! They can be read in any order, but the first published was *Haunts and Howls and Guardian Spells*. As I mentioned in the introduction, the very first Destiny Cats novella was published in *Guardian Spells*. The two previous Destiny Cats stories, *Destiny Through the Cats Eyes* and *Hourglass Through the Cats Eyes*, are also published as standalone eBooks now as well—in case you just want to see where Erica and Galahad started their journey.

As a side note, Jilly and Memnon are two of my favorite secondary characters and so, yes, I will likely be exploring more of their history in future Destiny Cats stories.

If you'd like to learn more about my fiction and keep up-to-date on what's happening and what's coming out, the best ways to do that are to visit my website, my store, or join my author newsletter. The website is updated monthly with news. The store has reading order lists, book sales, merch, and twice a month, I post a free short story in The Café. My author newsletter lands in your inbox directly. I send it out about once a month. And all new subscribers get two free stories that are only available to my newsletter people.

You can also follow my author page at BookBub, Facebook, or any of your favorite vendors. And I do spend a little time (*cough, maybe more than a little, cough*) on social media. As I write this, mostly Bluesky and Instagram. I also love hearing from readers, so don't be shy about emailing!

Thanks again for reading *Haunts and Howls and Dragon Tales*!

Don't Miss
A Single

HAUNT AND HOWL

From
KAT SIMONS

BOOKS BY KAT SIMONS

Haunts and Howls Collections

Haunts and Howls and Guardian Spells

Haunts and Howls Where Demons Dwell

Haunts and Howls and Jesters Bells

Haunts and Howls and Fairy Dales

Haunts and Howls and Dragon Tales

Destiny Cats Series

Destiny Through the Cats Eyes

Hourglass Through the Cats Eyes

Pick Your Genre Collections

Who Steals a Dragon

Joan of Kerry Series

Joan of Kerry: Joan and the Abhartach

Joan and the Leprechaun

Joan and the Kraken

Joan and the Selkie

Joan and the Goblins

Paranormal Romance

Dragon Thief Series

Seven Families: Wolf Series

Tiger Shifters Series

Romancing the Leopard: A Tiger Shifters-Cary Redmond Crossover Novel

Urban Fantasy

The Cary Redmond Series

Cary Redmond Short Stories and Collections

Demon Witch Series

Friday's Curious Shop Series

Contemporary Fantasy

**Tombstone Wizard * The Unshattered Sword * Going Out of Business: Everything's for Sale * Anger Management * Demonic Dates * The Museum of Small Art's Everyman * Burning Inside a Stone Circle * Bored Questless * I Just Ate a Bug * Ting Ling * Sophie Saves the World * Black Water Hawthorns * To Dance in Fallow Fields at Midnight * The Troll and the Dressmaker*

Stories from the Café

The Café Collections

Stories from the Café: Volume One

Contemporary Romances

Designed for You

Poinsettias and Possibilities

Mystery and Thriller

ROSS AND **O**'N**EILL** **A**DVENTURES

Galileo's Pendulum

PERCY **J**AMES **M**YSTERIES

Movies May Murder

Cookies Can't Crime

Diamonds Do Damage

Replicas Risk Ruin

Vacation Deadly: An Action Adventure Thriller Collection

About the Author

Kat Simons earned her Ph.D. in animal behavior, working with animals as diverse as dolphins and deer. She brought her experience and knowledge of biology to her paranormal romance and urban fantasy fiction, where she delights in taking nature and turning it on its ear. She writes urban fantasy, contemporary fantasy, and paranormal romance in series which combine action adventure, the otherworldly, and a frequent dose of sexy romance.

The newest book in her bestselling romantic urban fantasy series about Protector Cary Redmond, The Trouble with Shifters and Fae Courts, sees a new direction for the intrepid Protector, her sexy leopard shifter mate, and the entire crew. Kat also launched a new novella length Urban Fantasy Romance series that follows the adventures of a magical thief and the dragon shifter prince she just can't seem to shake—and really doesn't want to. The first season of the Dragon Thief series released throughout 2024. Season Two begins in 2025 with The Crown of Kingship Job.

For something a little different, Kat also publishes fantasy, science fiction, and the occasional hockey romance under the name Isabo Kelly (https://www.isabokelly.com).

After traveling the world, living in places like Hawaii, Germany, and Ireland, Kat now lives in New York City with her family and a library's worth of books.

For more on Kat and her future books

Website: https://www.katsimons.com/
Newsletter: https://bit.ly/KatSimonsNewsletter

KatSimonsBooks

https://www.katsimonsbooks.com
https://www.TheCafeatKatSimonsBooks.com

Social Media

Facebook Page: https://www.facebook.com/
KatSimonsAuthor
BookBub: https://www.bookbub.com/authors/kat-
simons
Bluesky: https://bsky.app/profile/katsimons.bsky.
social
Instagram: https://www.instagram.com/isabokelly/
Threads: https://www.threads.net/@isabokelly

KATSIMONSBOOKS

Urban Fantasy

Romance

Mystery

And More!

KatSimonsBooks.Com

www.ingramcontent.com/pod-product-compliance
Lightning Source LLC
Chambersburg PA
CBHW021341310726